PUFFIN

THE TALKING BOOK: THE WILD JOURNEY OF COMMUNICATION—FROM CAVEMAN TO AI

Jane De Suza is the award-winning author of ten books and is published internationally. She writes with humour and sensitivity about the challenges facing children. Her books include *When the World Went Dark* (*When Impossible Happens* in the US and UK), *Flyaway Boy, The Midnight Years, Uncool* and the SuperZero series. An MBA, creative director, film writer and columnist for leading publications, she currently lives in Singapore.

ALSO IN PUFFIN BY JANE DE SUZA

Superzero and the Grumpy Ghosts
Superzero and the Clone Crisis
Flyaway Boy
When the World Went Dark

The Talking Book

The wild journey of communication—from caveman to AI.

JANE DE SUZA

Illustrations by **Siddhi Vartak**

PUFFIN BOOKS

An imprint of Penguin Random House

PUFFIN BOOKS

USA | Canada | UK | Ireland | Australia
New Zealand | India | South Africa | China | Singapore

Puffin Books is part of the Penguin Random House group of companies
whose addresses can be found at global.penguinrandomhouse.com

Published by Penguin Random House India Pvt. Ltd
4th Floor, Capital Tower 1, MG Road,
Gurugram 122 002, Haryana, India

Penguin
Random House
India

First published in Puffin Books by Penguin Random House India 2024

Text copyright © Jane De Suza 2024
Illustrations copyright © Siddhi Vartak 2024

ISBN 9780143463542

Book design and layout by Samar Bansal
Typeset in FS Me by Manipal Technologies Limited, Manipal

www.penguin.co.in

for Omalloor Gopalakrishnan,
Malayalam playwright, teacher and poet

CONTENTS

WORDS TO LANGUAGE

HUMANS WIRED TO SPEAK

NON-HUMAN LANGUAGE

EXPERIMENTS AND RECORDS

BEFORE WE BEGIN

As the sun sets, I set out to walk by the sea. I find a sandcastle abandoned halfway. A key. A family of sunbathing otters. An umbrella spinning on its own. A scuttling crab. A circling hawk. A fishing pole with no one fishing. Each has a story.

That's what this book brings you. Not crabs or otters, no. This is a collection of the bizarre, shimmering things buried in the path that language took. We'll pick them out together and let them tell their stories. These mysterious, hilarious stories that make our minds tick, our jaws drop, and raise as many questions as the ones answered.

To start with, why can't a chimp that shares 98% of our DNA talk? How did humans share secrets in public? Where do a thousand new words a year appear from, and where were they hiding earlier? Will we, one day, talk without speaking?

There is no rigid, linear roadmap of how languages grew. It is a sea with changing tides and yet-undiscovered treasures. Every once in a while, a new find or theory pops up, and though I've cross-checked each story with multiple sources, scholars of language don't always agree.

While research forms the backbone of this book, the storytelling takes creative licence. Dogs cannot talk. And kids cannot time travel. Except in our minds and through our words, and without words there would be only . . .

Jane De Suza,
Singapore, October 2023

HOW IT ALL BEGAN

On a Dark Night
No One Speaks of

A fire blazes inside the small cave. Its crackling keeps the sounds of the night away, out beyond the thick, impenetrable foliage, where they belong. Children, their hair long and matted, caked in mud with teeth sharp and eyes darting, huddle around their strong, muscled mothers, burrowing in for warmth and protection; sometimes handed a shred of meat, sometimes swatted away.

Without warning, a guttural scream pierces the still of the night. The ragged panting and thudding of running steps draw closer, followed by a panicked crashing through the last shreds of undergrowth that keep the cave hidden. Breaking through the final few bushes, a male heaves himself in. With the whites of his eyes shimmering and his face contorted, he looms over the small group. His long-nailed fingers, grimy and bloodied, curl themselves into talons. He bares his teeth and snarls. As the group crawls away, curling into one giant feral ball, he pounces at the youngest child and picks her up by a frail arm. Then he lifts a burning branch from the fire with his other hand. He pivots, swirling around, the burning branch hoisted above him, and snarls while the others cower. The flames cast long shadows on the walls of the cave, magnifying the terror.

Close your eyes and picture yourself as that child in that cave, 200,000 years ago.

It would be wiser to open your eyes now, actually, to read the rest.

There are questions you must ask urgently—your life depends on them, but you can't. You don't know how to. You can't speak.

Is this new entrant going to harm you or help you? Is he angry or frightened? Is he hungry? What do his curling hands mean? Is he warning you about a thunderstorm? Or an attacking group? Or . . . too late! In a piercing roar, a flash of fiery orange fur and long, sharp yellow claws leap in from the dark—a sabre-toothed tiger in all its fury. So that's what he was trying to tell you about.

We'll never know how the story ends for this small family of early Hominins. They could never tell us. It's not hard to see that this is why we started to speak. We would die without it.

Now that we've got the why out of the way, where and when did we start speaking?

The Hunt for Great Grandma

The trek to find our earliest known relative takes us to the land of great thirst, where, today, the black-maned Kalahari lion sits under the shade of a single tree, his tail batting away flies in the baking heat of the day. For miles and miles, the sandy desert sprawls out as far as the eye can see. Wildebeest, hyenas and leopards, all lurk at a safe distance from the king of the Kalahari.

The desert's name is taken from *Kgala*, a Tswana word that translates as great thirst. Although, 200,000 years ago, it was quite the opposite. The terrain was waterlogged with wetlands, lakes and swamps. In this Makgadikgadi wetland, a woman roamed, hunted, grunted, raised children and taught genetics to billions who were not yet born. She was not the first human who lived, but certainly the first known human we could trace ourselves back to. Your great, great (many times over) grandmother and mine too. So, even though I don't know who you are, I know this about you—we're related.

Our grand old matriarch goes by the nickname Mitochondrial Eve. An unbroken line of daughters, from whom we originally evolved, can be traced back to her. That makes each one of us on this planet today distant cousins. So, go ahead and put your favourite film star in your family tree.

Now for the deeper mystery: the great, great (many times over) grandmother has never been found. How, then, do we know she existed in this land before time?

A DETECTIVE STORY THAT GOES BACKWARDS

Who was Mitochondrial Eve? No one had seen her and lived to tell the tale. There wasn't a body either. Where was the proof of existence?

Genetic scientists donned their detective hats, and over time, through trial and error, they investigated the secret codes held within our mitochondrial DNA. The unique genetic sequences in our mitochondria passed down from mother to daughter can trace our matrilineal history through several generations.

In a massive hunt, multiple suspects were brought in, hundreds of samples taken and commonalities and differences laid bare.

Finally—a breakthrough! A clue that was hidden in plain sight, something everyone had but didn't know: a specific DNA sequence that all humans have in common today. The geneticists had to dig out where this DNA sequence originated. They needed to find the initial scene. What, after all, is a good detective story without a scene?

As humans migrated, the initial lineage underwent changes and modifications that diluted the genetic code. But where did it all begin? In a dramatic finale, after sifting through many different populations, the closest and most unchanged sequences of the DNA lineage were revealed to belong to an indigenous group in Africa. This continent, then, was our earliest homeland. The home of our great, great (many times over) grandmother, our common progenitor, Mitochondrial Eve. A home that is guarded by the black-maned Kalahari lion today. Perhaps he knows just how precious the land is.

If all of us have descended from one female, shouldn't we all be speaking her language?

Speechless Stories

Mitochondrial Eve would have gladly passed on her language, but she didn't have one. The earliest migrants were Hominins who hadn't begun speaking yet. They explored the planet walking, not talking. Yet, they are an indelible part of our language history and can help us understand how each of us landed up in a different pocket of the world and created our speech there.

Out of Africa, they trekked—the descendants of the great mother, our ancestors, the hunters, gatherers, explorers, inventors—for food, after prey and away from attackers.

From their lands, they kept moving towards that elusive line—the horizon—and it kept moving away. Was it alive? Each time, the small units moved their home sites a little further. And then further again. It took oodles of courage. They came up against dense forests that swallowed the light and swamps that gobbled beings alive, yet they ventured into them with no idea of what lay beyond. Just the grit to keep moving.

Out of Africa, they moved across Europe and Asia to be sledgehammered by the bitter cold and sheets of ice. Back then, many of the larger land masses were fused together. So, our ancestors continued on foot till the point where land ended and the seas began. Incredibly, they even crossed the seas (the water levels used to be lower at that time) to Oceania and later to the Americas. Last on the globe-trotting itinerary were the Arctic lands.

THE EARLIEST TRAVEL DIARIES

Accounts of the first migrations are being uncovered even today with each new excavation of an ancient site revealing a little more. Piece by piece, scientists are putting together stories that had been asleep for centuries. Weapons and tools dug out from underground hiding places narrate tales of eating, fighting, hunting, swimming, but none of speaking.

The initial travellers out of Africa took everything with them except language. And yet, they told their stories. Stories of where they travelled, the routes they took, what they did in the places they took shelter in, how they lived and how they died. They even told stories of how they were related.

STORIES BURIED UNDER ASH

One of the most explosive stories tells of how the ground shuddered and ripped apart. Fire shot out of the earth's belly and into the skies, burning them red.

About 75,000 years ago, a violent volcanic eruption in Toba, Indonesia, shook the lands and seas for thousands of miles around. It covered every living thing in molten lava and heralded the beginning of a long winter. Long? A winter that lasted seven years.

Eons later, archaeologists on an excavation site in Jwalapuram in Andhra Pradesh discovered buried secrets. Under several layers of volcanic debris, ash and rock, they found tools related to those used in Africa during the same period. It was proof of travel as strong as any flight ticket today and proof of one of the earliest settlements outside Africa. Tools, bones, weapons and utensils were carried to newer lands. The trail these left are our storytellers today, still speechless at this point.

Isn't it time that someone started speaking?

Bow-wow or Pooh-pooh?

LET'S START TALKING ABOUT HOW WE STARTED TALKING

It was impossible to capture sound from hundreds of thousands of years ago, and since nobody invented that time-machine, there were no definite answers to how we started speaking. Discussions grew deafening and confusing, and arguments violent. Letters and papers piled up and toppled over. Theories were raised and shot down.

When it grew too quarrelsome, talking began, and talking about it was over! The Linguistic Society of Paris in 1886, founded for the very purpose of studying language, banned talking about how talking began. The ban, like most bans, was lifted later. But bans are temperamental things, and before someone bans something again, here, quickly, are the most fun theories:

Please note: Max Mueller, famed linguist and Indologist, can be credited (or blamed) for some of the whimsical names for the origin of language theories.

The bow-wow theory: The next time you're in a zoo, notice what people do. Not the animals, but the people. They stand outside cages and roar at the tigers, chatter at the monkeys and cluck at the ducks. None of the animals are impressed. *You should be in the cages*, is what their bored expressions say. This mimicking yielded the bow-wow theory. German philosopher, Johann Gottfried von Herder, first proposed the idea that humans began to speak by mimicking the sounds that animals made.

The pooh-pooh theory: Danish linguist Otto Jespersen asked if language could have evolved from exclamations of surprise, pain or pleasure, like ow! Phew! Ha, ha! But then, how would I write this book in a series of oops and aarghs?

The ta-ta theory: This theory waved itself goodbye. In 1930, influenced by Darwin, Sir Richard Paget said that sounds mimicked gestures. When you say 'ta-ta', your tongue is waving the same way your hand does. But then why doesn't the tongue do the same for ciao or *phir milenge* or see you later, alligator?

Tofa; tạm biệt; paalam; nagemist; sayonara; zài jiàn; selamat jalan; usale kahle; gorusuruz; kwaheri—that's waving ta-ta in different tongues.

Onomatopoeia theory: This proposes that a word originates from its sound, like splash, boom, zoom, tick tock, fizz, flush and buzz. Every language has them. Among Hindi's more imaginative ones is *kheench*, the sound of something being pulled. Your tooth that's being pulled out or the chalk dragged across the board. *Pharpharahat* is the sound of a bird flapping its wings and *gadgadaahat* is that of thunder. If this were true, then how did words bubble up for things that had no sound? Air, silence and sound itself. Explain that, onomatopoetic!

Darwin and the Dinner Plate

The Australia Zoo's longstanding claim is that its longstanding tortoise, Harriet, was brought over from the Galapagos Islands to England by Charles Darwin.

Hatched around 1830, she had grown from the size of a dinner plate to the size of a dinner table when she passed on in 2006. Neither Darwin nor Harriet can now verify this claim of friendship. Harriet, of course, never spoke about it or about anything at all, but Darwin said quite a bit, especially about where in the chain of evolution humans began to speak.

Darwin's step theory: Charles Darwin will forever be the man who shook up our belief systems through his theory of evolution. In his book *The Descent of Man*, 1871, Darwin says that language is just another step in our evolution from animals. Surely the snarls and growls of early communication were warnings imitating other predators? (Wonder how that story on Page 3 ended finally?)

An infant's babbling sounds like birdsong. Your mother raves about how melodious you sounded as a baby, though your neighbours complained you were as noisy as a malfunctioning electric drill.

Was there a magic moment?

Most of the theories above are theories of continuity to explain the slow evolution of language from gestures or noises. Since nothing in this field goes down easy, there are also theories of discontinuity from those who think that humans struck gold in the talking department—Ka-Ching!—one fine day, rather through one fine gene.

The FOXP2 gene: human, not fox

'Talking is hardwired into our brains,' said Noam Chomsky, a revered name in linguistics. Human babies are born with language ability and animals aren't. A happy little single gene mutation, just one, thousands of years ago, enabled human beings to speak.

The good news: Does this mean we have one mutant ancestor to thank for language?

The bad news: Does this also mean that speaking was just an accident? Had the gene not gone rogue, we'd probably still be grunting.

Later research offered more proof. The FOXP2 gene, linked to language, is marginally different in humans and chimpanzees, who otherwise share roughly 98% of DNA. This mutation enabled humans to speak. Sadly, foxes, despite all the fables, never did.

The fox comes from the dog family, Canidae. So why don't they just call this talking gene a dog gene?

The First Word

Pull out your babyhood videos. That babbling, drooling infant with fingers in the mouth—that is you. Your mother bends over you, holding your mash in a bowl, when suddenly, you smack your lips together and blabber, spit bubbles and all, 'Mmm . . . aaa . . .' and she melts—tears and laughter blending. She'd cartwheel if she wasn't holding the bowl, because she would then need to clean the mash off the ceiling, really. Overjoyed at this response to your performance, and, of course, with absolutely no idea why, you repeat the magic mantra, 'Mamamama'. You keep smacking your lips together with no clue that it's your name for her, but it makes her happy, and that makes you happy.

Your first word, according to many scholars, would get the most votes for the first word ever spoken. It is the sound of babies suckling, of eating, of kisses. It is no coincidence that almost every language has a word for the word mother with an 'M' in it.

Mutti, mai, mama, amma, mor, maminka, ma, mana, mei, mati, mum, mom, mam-depending on where you grew up in the world, that's what you'd call your delighted mother. Unless, of course, your first words are Papa or Puppy, which is just plain ungrateful, and Mama's not going to do cartwheels over that, for sure.

Grandmothers tell completely different (and more exciting) stories about how language came to be. Let's add those in.

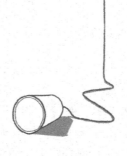

God's Gifts

Divine source theories about the origins of language from across religions and cultures say pooh-pooh! to fox genes.

1. The egg came first

There was only one tribe—ours, and only one language—ours. Then someone went and ate two hummingbird eggs. Bad move! That immediately led to the tribe splintering, with each group running off in a different direction and speaking a new language. What about the egg-eater? No idea.

2. Bamboo babies

The first couple grew out of the original being, the horned giant Pangu. Their excitement about being the first couple soon waned because their three children couldn't speak. They prayed hard and long, and finally the gods granted their wish. The gods were creative in those days, even in granting wishes. They instructed the father to cut a bamboo cane into three and told the mother to light a fire. When the three bits of bamboo were thrown into the fire, the children began to suddenly cry out in different tongues. We are not very sure what the parents said, but, then, parents usually understand whatever their kids say, so all was well, we assume.

3. Goddess of the Wise

When Lord Brahma was meditating while creating the universe, his mind expanded and grew and out of this was born a girl. Upon her, he bestowed the title of Saraswati: the goddess of communication-learning, knowledge, music, and, in her avatar as *Vac*, of speech. That is why, on the day of Saraswati puja, children place their books at the feet of the goddess's idol.

4. A prehistoric high-rise

Many stories start with enormous floods. In this case, the survivors decided to build a massive tower touching the heavens. The presumptuousness! Touch the heavens, huh? God decided to teach them a lesson and got them all babbling in different languages, with no one understanding the other. Without communication, their ambitious tower couldn't be built. This tower of Babel (linked to early Babylon) is the reason why people speak different languages today.

5. Mountain-makers

This time, both a flood and a big tower—well, a pyramid, actually—the (first) Great Pyramid of Cholula, also called the artificial mountain; like anyone but God could create a mountain. These people! Honestly, who did they think they were? So what if they were twelve-foot giants? This time around, the gods were so furious that they hurled fire down from above and burnt the pyramid to ashes, and perhaps some giants too.

6. Three from the tree

Once, when the sons of Borr, Odin, Vili and Ve were out on a walk, they came across some trees. Normally, young lads would climb those trees or click selfies against them. But these boys shaped men out of the trees. Eager to arm their latest creations, they gifted them powers. The gifts of speech, sight and hearing were gifted by Borr's third son, Ve.

Talking like mad

We learnt to speak because we were all mad, literally. The population spoke only one language till a terrible famine swept across the earth. People, starved and sick, went mad. This madness drove them from one place to the other, across the world, babbling as they did so. Their mindless chatter soon became the origin of words in each language.

The last laugh

A blood-thirsty one, this tale. Skip it if you're having lunch. Wurruri was an irritating old woman who wandered around striking out fires that kept sleeping people warm, all the while cackling gleefully. When she died, the other people had the last laugh. Each group of people that ate a different part of her remains began to speak in a different language and wandered off to a different part of the world.

Now that we've got to the end, let's tell you where these stories come from. I love happy endings.

1. The Ticuna Tribe of the Amazon
2. Chinese mythology
3. A Hindu scripture, the Brahmana Purana
4. The Bible, book of Genesis
5. A Mexican legend
6. Norse mythology
7. The Bantu people of West Africa
8. The Indigenous people of Encounter Bay, Australia

How can we know how the earliest humans communicated when we weren't there?

FROM TALKING TO WRITING

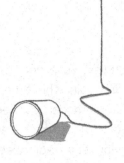

Diary of
a Caveman

The earliest Hominins rocked! And we know this without being there because . . . ? Well, they recorded their daily lives on the walls of their homes—on rocks. Cave people left signs, etches and sketches of what they'd been up to. Here a spear, there a deer. They communicated with each other and with us, who entered the picture centuries later.

#FirstRock. The Blombos cave in Africa had been naturally sealed off because of rising and falling water levels and was discovered only recently. In it lay something more precious than shipwrecked treasure. A piece of rock. The hashtag of criss-cross lines etched in ochre on a piece of rock spoke of a bored artist grabbing a bit of rest in that cave. 73,000 years ago. #firstdrawing #rockartrocks.

Art made on rocks and caves continues to turn up at different archaeological sites even today, each adding a new piece to the jigsaw of what we know of long-ago lives.

One of the earliest cave paintings was found in the Maltravieso cave in Spain. This time, we can't credit our ancestors for it. It was made by a Neanderthal, a different species of the early Hominin that died out. Before exiting, they left their handprints on walls, deep in caves and nooks that were exceptionally difficult to get into. That was 64,000 years ago. 'I was here,' the hands seem to declare. Or, maybe, 'Hello there, strange modern people who can't climb trees.' Or, perhaps, 'Bye for now, I'll be back.' Gulp!

Rock artists portrayed life around them, and it was not all human. The earliest animal to be captured in a portrait was a pig, drawn in the Sulawesi caves of Indonesia about 45,000 years ago.

The first drawing was of a pig? A pig? I am man's best friend. And they first draw a pig?

At some point, the ancients went beyond the chronicles of mundane everyday life and into a world of spirits that their imaginations had conjured.

The earliest fantasy art prize goes to the Lascaux caves in France. There is an image on the wall inside that looks very much like a unicorn and another that is thought to be a wizard.

The reason cave art continues to be found in dribs and drabs over time is because the caves were well-hidden by the changes that the planet underwent. The Lascaux caves were closed in by a landslide around 13,000 BCE, and discovered in modern times, quite accidentally, by teenagers who followed their dog in.

I have been running after my dog, Marcopolo, for years, and he never led me to anything more interesting than old shoes. And to think we named him after an explorer.

Cave Popcorn

Warning: Not edible.

Cave popcorn may look like popcorn, but it doesn't taste like it. Those who tasted it haven't survived to tell the tale. It's the calcium carbonate lumps and bumps that cling to cave walls. As mineral layers get deposited on the walls and on the painting on these walls, they draw in uranium, which decays into thorium at a given rate. Uranium-thorium dating can scientifically identify how old a cave painting is. The popcorn can be dated even when the paint on the walls can't.

HIDDEN IN THE HILLS OF INDIA

The Aravalli range of mountains in North India kept their own cave art secret for centuries. They were well-shrouded, high and deep in the forests, known only to the locals and far from the prying eye of any outsider.

Now, scientists have discovered cave paintings among the many ancient sites in the region and dated some of them to be almost 20,000 years old. Even more thrilling, the art itself is a proper class in history. Many artists over different eras used these walls as their canvas. As the art moved onwards from the Stone Age and hands and imaginations grew more skilled, they progressed from simple to elaborate, from lines to shapes and from animals to stick drawings of themselves.

Pocket Calendars

'Smart young inventors have come up with the latest technology of the age: small, light, portable tracking devices'—a news headline you would stumble across in the twenty-first century or in 30,000 BCE?

The ancients realized that hunting big game was dependent on time and day. Would a shimmering moonlit night be better to see their prey? Or would the darkness offer more cover? What if they themselves counted as prey in the dark? Would they step on a lurking snake? They created their own calendars to track the moon's phases, in which the moon itself moves in snake-like patterns. It was pointless etching out these calendars on their walls at home for their families to stare at; they were needed on the hunt. Therefore, the etchings were marked on bone or stone which could be easily carried around. Pocket calendars long before there were pockets.

Did art evolve into writing?

Emojis from 3,000 Years Ago

Was that the first writing? Pictures on cave walls? Experts can't quite agree on whether pictures count as language. A picture paints a thousand words, some say. But your mother probably says, 'Don't send me a smiley; write instead.' What would you say? Are emojis a kind of language?

While you chew on that, we'll talk about bulls. Bulls will demonstrate one way in which pictures can form written communication.

WHEN A BULL IS NOT A BULL

Bulls were drawn on walls. Bulls were drawn inside caves. Bulls were drawn charging or fighting. That's art.

Sometimes, the bull was not a bull. Say, a specific community wanted to denote that its king or god was strong and powerful, they may have depicted him with the symbol of a bull*. When you see that specific bull symbol, drawn the same way each time, you know it's about the king. Everyone in that community understands this symbol isn't a bull at all. Treason! It's your king.

A symbol or character is the basic unit of all written communication. That symbol, drawn in that same manner, signifies the same thing to everyone who understands that language. It can stand for a sound or a word; for example, 't' signifies a sound in the Latin alphabet but the number seven in Chinese.

Here are how writing systems use symbols:

Symbol = word: logographic writing system
Example: Chinese or hieroglyphs

Symbol = syllable: syllabary
Example: some Japanese, Indic or Greek scripts

Symbol = letter: The alphabetic system
Example: English and almost 100 others

* Among the rock inscriptions in the ancient Egyptian city of Elkab, archaeologists uncovered a panel with the symbol of a bull's head on a pole. It represented 'royal authority over the cosmos'. Both king and god, then.

The Y in English is, well, a 'Y'.
Why? You know why.
In Russian, the Y
sounds like an 'oo'.
Why? No, not why, but 'whoo'.
But the h in Russian
sounds like an 'n'.
Why? Not why.
Not 'whoo'.
Now it's a 'noo'!

So, who drew or wrote or signed . . .
or whatever—the first bull?

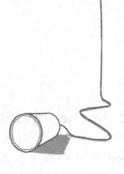

Laughing Tablets

The first person who ever wrote anything won't go down in history, but the first people will.

Civilizations across the world independently came up with their own system of recording things, each in their own land.

The early Sumerians began recording their transactions on cuneiform tablets way back in the fourth century BCE. In close competition with cuneiform were the Egyptian hieroglyphics and the Indus Valley script.

Why did they start writing? So that no one could, for example, claim later that they had got two eggs less because he said, or she said, or you said. It was all down there in writing. Those little squiggles found today on thousands of clay tablets are a record. A fly-on-the-wall look at people's daily lives, trades, wages, gifts, lists and even their fashions.

Tablet school

If you were a child from a wealthy family back then, you were sent off to school to be taught to write on clay tablets. You were taught the art of pressing a stylus made of reed, just so, on the little clay tablet. All sun-baked and permanent; no backspace key. In fact, if you made a mistake, some scholar from 5,000 years in the future would catch you out. The students made elaborate excuses to bunk class (nothing's changed, has it?) and more creative ones even to get parental sympathy.

Not fair, Mummy!

Iddin-Sin's unwittingly hilarious note on a clay tablet from the eighteenth century BCE is being chuckled over till today. The son of an aristocrat sent off to boarding school, Iddin-Sin, was trying some emotional blackmail on his mother. He claimed that she sent him no new clothes; he had only poor and scanty clothes, while his classmate received newer, fancier clothes. 'You do not love me,' he ended the note with a whine. We won't know whether the whine worked or not, since we haven't yet found his mother's reply.

More written records kept showing up over more digs. Some cuneiform tablets were even bound together so that messengers couldn't cheat and edit the accounts within them. Some of the funnier discoveries are coming up.

The lion's diet

Forty-five hundred years ago, a Sumerian official in Akkaka found himself with a lion. A real live lion, which he was worried wouldn't stay alive much longer. His cuneiform tablet to his lord details his sorry state. A lion had entered their loft. Far from worrying about the well-being of the people in the house, the official was agitated about the health of the lion. It was presented with a pig and a dog and refused to eat either (lucky animals!). Anxious about the self-imposed hunger strike of this self-invited guest, the official wrote that after five days, he had decided to have the lion shipped to his lord. We hope that both the lion and the lord (and the pig and the dog, and, of course, the stressed-out official) survived, but, once again, there is no response that has been found to this suspenseful story.

Four-thousand-year-old food

Moving on from a lion's food to that of humans, researchers from Yale University decided to try out a 4,000-year-old Mesopotamian lamb stew. None of them fell sick. Let's quickly add that the ingredients weren't that old. Only the recipe was.

The stew is made with meat, water, onions, garlic, leeks, salt, milk and dried barley cakes. That's all it says in about four lines on the cuneiform tablet.

Black humour

Humour, unlike stew, never grows stale. In this Akkadian tale from the first century BCE, a poor man of Nippur tried to impress the mayor and get invited to his banquet by gifting him a goat. The plan backfired. The mean mayor insulted him instead. The poor man wreaked revenge in a plot involving disguises, bloodshed and hahas aplenty.

The first graphic novel

The battle of Til Tuba between the Assyrians and the Elamites is depicted in gory detail on a massive stone, one of Mesopotamia's most significant finds. It is a story of victory because the Assyrians won. Not too sure they would have put it up on a six-by-six-foot wall if the battle had turned the other way. The stone shows heads being chopped off and arrows struck into soldiers. Look, it warns about what happens to those who dare go against our king.

Maths cheat sheet

The lines etched on an ancient postcard-sized Babylonian tablet, Plimpton 322, had scholars guessing till they eventually realized that it looked suspiciously like a math teacher's cheat code for homework. Possibly from way back, somewhere between 1900 and 1600 BCE.

38

Wildlife protection pillars

Emperor Ashoka's pillars from the third century BCE show him to be a kind, humane king who wanted his subjects to be the same. These edicts were inscribed in Prakrit, besides Greek and Aramaic (to cater to the people of all the lands he governed). 'Be good, be generous, be kind to animals,' the writings declared. Ashoka included a long list of animals that shouldn't be killed for food or burnt in forest fires or fed to other animals. And if people still did? What if you went ahead and killed a deer? So not fine! A fine of 100 *panas* for you!

Lice were never nice

This has got to be the creepy-crawliest. An ivory comb found in Israel has the first complete sentence, written in Canaanite from 1700 BCE. It says, 'May this tusk root out the lice of the hair and the beard.'

The longest lasting love

This love song has made it to the charts 4,000 years later. 'Istanbul #2461' is the love song dedicated to Sumerian King Shu-Sin of the third dynasty of Ur. It is proof of the love of the poetess for the king, but who exactly was she?

The love song is written by Shu-Sin's bride, and here's where it gets mystical. This marriage was part of a sacred ritual where the king married the goddess Inanna every

spring. Was this written by a human or a goddess, then? Some detective work is needed there. And here's some excellent digging already done.

A crook caught centuries later

The buried city of Ur uncovered a cheat who will never be forgotten. Ea-Nasir, the trader himself, wasn't excavated, but archaeologists stumbled upon a collection of complaints in his house, all etched on cuneiform tablets. Like most men keep trophies, Ea-Nasir kept his pile of complaints safe.

Most of the complainants are agitated about giving Ea-Nasir silver and getting bad copper in return. Whether Ea-Nasir gave them all better copper as compensation is a mystery that remains buried, but we think not. He turned to selling second-hand clothes next.

The next time an adult tells you to stop complaining, tell them about the complaints that have survived for centuries. Threaten to etch yours into clay and bake it too.

Could the moderns crack all the ancient scripts?

Code Crackers Wanted

It's 2,000 BCE and baking hot outside. Your tiny house with its low, flat roof is like an oven, so you're outdoors. The wealthy trader nearby has a house with a courtyard, and his kids play inside it. But you . . . you have the wide, open spaces. You throw what you're eating to a bunch of dogs. They are hunting dogs, but they roam around the place, and you like playing with them when your father's not looking.

You see your friend pulling along a toy on wheels. You pester him to give you a chance. He refuses, and you try to snatch it. He pounces at you, and in the middle of the scuffle, you hear a gruff shout. 'You're up to all sorts of mischief' you're told. 'Time to get to work. Children need to work hard. Do you think life is all fun and games? You belong to the Indus Valley Civilization, not some futuristic sci-fi twenty-first century.'

You stomp behind your older siblings, making sure they know how grouchy you are to help in the farming, flicking the sweat off your chin and squinting at the sun. Next year, perhaps, when you're older, they'll take you on the hunt, and your mother will tie a small amulet around your arm to keep you safe. What amulet? What does it say?

The flourishing Indus Valley Civilization was at its peak between 2,600 and 1,900 BCE and spread across the Indo-Pakistan territories. Almost sixty excavation sites along the river Indus have yielded a wealth of inscribed objects, roughly 4,000 at last count. Inscriptions have been found on seals, pottery, tools and weapons.

Think of it as a gigantic jigsaw puzzle. Scholars have to put together the various objects, pick out all the signs on them, compare them, and then crack the code. Over 100 exhaustive scholarly attempts have already been made. Leading studies include those of Indologist Asko Parpola and epigrapher Iravatham Mahadevan, a leading name in the field. Both their studies have pointed to about 400 distinguishable signs.

The square seals found were inscribed with script and animals. Elephants, tigers, rhinos, buffaloes, crocodiles and most exhilarating—from a 4,000-year-old seal at Mohenjo-Daro—the famed Indus unicorn!

These seals were probably used to imprint on clay as official stamps for trade or administration but some more exciting uses are suspected, too. Perhaps, some were used as talismans or amulets you could wear, to woo a good spiritual power or to ward off an evil one. Some even get into storytelling through depictions of animals and other not-quite-worldly beings. The writing was from right to left. How can we know that today without any video proof? Here's one clue. On a few seals, the symbols on the left got increasingly squashed—exactly what you do when you start off writing big and fancy and then end up trying to squeeze the tail of your sentence into the remaining space.

THE HACKATHON IS ON!

The Indus script hasn't been deciphered completely. The decoding of most other scripts is due to bilingual connections. They are similar to the languages in use today.

The Indus script isn't mirrored in any Indian script, not in Devanagari, Bengali or Brahmi . . . no slashes or dashes or curves or curls that mean anything in any language today. As the Indus Valley Civilization died out, sadly, so did their writing systems.

The few core signs, around thirty, that all the inscriptions together display are also a problem. Other signs are just adaptations of these main ones. It's tough to find patterns that could suggest meanings when there are only a few. We need more.

Any passionate explorers, diggers, archaeologists or linguists out there? Any puzzle-lovers, codebreakers or challenge-seekers who would like to give it a shot?

I am a passionate digger.
Also, they found terracotta dog figurines in the Indus Valley sites. You forgot to say that.

How did the first few words turn into so many languages?

WORDS
TO LANGUAGE

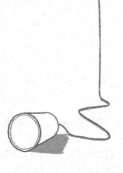

Travelling Tongues

'Remember to take your spear . . . and your cooking pot . . . and, oh yes, the baby. Don't forget the baby.' Humans moved and carried their kids, their weapons, their colds and coughs, their bites and mites, and their annoying habits. And their language? When did they begin to carry their language with them?

When exactly language began is still murky territory. After all, the pots and pans and tools hadn't captured voices. Scientists needed to turn to other clues, such as fossils and bones. Did we have the vocal apparatus necessary for talking? From the shape of the vocal tract, it is assumed that we couldn't talk until about 100,000 or 150,000 years ago when the first modern humans emerged. Somewhere in that period lies ground zero for language.

Human migrations after this point saw language hop on for the ride with the other baggage. Wave after wave of migrations hit newer lands. When the new entrants met earlier inhabitants of those lands, they either merged or forced the others out. The Neanderthals, though earlier along the Hominin evolution chain, were driven into extinction by our own ancestors, the Homo sapiens.

Over time, as people travelled and met others, languages began to get tossed about like veggies in a stew. New languages emerged; some morphed, some mixed, some merged and some melted away. The people had to adapt. 'Oh, if that's your word for tiger, I'll use that now. Because there's a tiger right behind you.'

PROTOLANGUAGES

These the few original languages which have spawned multiple others. Languages that share a common root are of the same language family. A new language born into this family is called a daughter language. The few original protolanguages have given rise to at least 7,000 recorded languages today.

Here are some of the roots of the languages we're familiar with currently.

Indo-European

Hindi and English come from the same protolanguage. Surprised? It's also the one with the most speakers in the world. The Indo-European protolanguage trickled down from the Neolithic or New Stone Age. The first languages to spark off from here were Sanskrit, Greek and Latin. Loads of other languages followed from these: Russian, Bengali, French, Punjabi, *ityaadi*.

Sino-Tibetan

Chinese, Burmese and Tibetan are descendants of the Sino-Tibetan protolanguage. This protolanguage also wins honours for creating the language with the most native speakers in the world: Chinese, including its dialects.

Niger-Congo

This protolanguage proudly parades the most daughters. 1,524 daughter languages, including Swahili, Yoruba and Fula.

Austronesian

Once the largest family in the world, today around 20% of the world's population speaks one of these languages, like Malay, Javanese, Tagalog or Sundanese.

Dravidian

Southern India has a distinct language tradition which goes back centuries and tells its own story. Unlike the languages

of the North, the South Indian languages do not come from the Indo-European protolanguage, though there were many overlaps with Sanskrit later on. With a long, strong cultural and literary history, Tamil, Telegu, Malayalam and Kannada, among several others, have grown from here.

Brahui Brothers

Secreted away in the chill, windswept, high hills of Baluchistan is a tribe of sheep-herding nomads who speak in a tongue unrelated to those around them. The people of this ethnic tribe have spoken Brahui for centuries. Brahui descends from the Dravidian protolanguage, unlike the languages in the rest of the region. In fact, many scholars feel that the people of this tribe are the caretakers of a Dravidian language handed down by the ancient Harappan population, way back when the Indus Valley Civilization reigned supreme over these lands.

FUNNY FACT, I.E., IF YOU FIND ROMANCE FUNNY

French, Spanish, Portuguese and Italian belong to the Romance language family. Because they sound romantic?

That's what some would have you believe. But here's the secret: 'Romance' comes from the word Roman (Latin), from which these languages evolved.

SOLO RIDERS

Like always, there are some who refuse to join any gang. Proud outliers, protective of their distinct heritage. Those who don't fall into any language families are called language isolates. Though many isolates are endangered because they are spoken by small, secluded tribes, a thriving isolate with millions of speakers today is Korean.

NINETEEN-THOUSAND WAYS TO SAY ANYTHING

Papua New Guinea is home to many protected tribes who have fiercely safeguarded their mother tongues. This gives this cluster of islands a jaw-dropping 800 languages for a small population of 10 million, making this country the most linguistically diverse in the world.

Another staggering fact from closer home. The Indian Ministry of Education has listed twenty-two official languages in India and at least four main language families: Indo-European, Dravidian, Austro-Asiatic and Sino-Tibetan.

According to the census commissioner, raw data from the last census recorded 19,569 mother tongues, rich in variations and dialects. These were further clubbed together and replications removed to arrive at an astonishing 121 languages spoken by over 10,000 people each. We can proudly claim that ours is a land of diversity like no other.

The Three-hour-long Word

Languages grew in their own peculiar ways. Some languages, like Sanskrit and German, hitched words together to create compound words that are almost as long as sentences.

Sanskrit wins the award for the longest word in any language—a 195-letter word used by Tirumalamba, a poet of the Vijayanagara empire.

The longest word ever outside a language belongs in a lab. It's the chemical name of a protein which starts like this: methionylthreonylglu . . . It takes about three hours to say it all and fifty pages to write it down. And if that makes you shudder, you may just have hippopotomonstrosesquippedaliophobia, a long word which means you have a fear of long words.

You'd think it meant a fear of hippos. But there is no word that conveys a fear of hippos. Hippophobia is a fear of horses.

When there's a bunch of languages acting like a bunch of hooligans, what do they need next?

No It
Sense Makes

The Oxford Dictionary defines language as the principal method of human communication, consisting of words used in a structured and conventional way and conveyed by speech, writing or gesture. (So, are emojis a language or not?) In short, a language is not a bunch of words rampaging around willy-nilly. It needs rules, grammar and vocabulary. You can't use the words however you feel like. There is an order in which you place them. Or sense makes it no? Exactly! Or it makes no sense.

THE BOOK OF EIGHT

An ant scrambled in the dusty mud, almost turning turtle. (A favour the turtle couldn't return because it never turned ant.) The tiny ant, hoisting a burden twice its size, scurried to join the end of a queue of other hardworking ants. A young boy bent over it, his knees and elbows digging into the sand, his mouth agape. The guru shut his tired eyes and sighed. For over two hours, his pupils had sat in the baking sun, with only a single leafy tree to shield them all, reciting after him. The ones in front were bright-eyed, but there at the back, that dreamy one had his nose buried in the sand, another was agog at the chirping of a bird in the tree above and two others were squabbling. Would they remember the lesson? Would they appreciate the value of what they were being taught to pass on to their own children someday?

While mothers oiled their children's hair, while bright-eyed students rocked at the feet of their masters, while priests began narrations in temples, they had one thing in common—none of it was written down. They sang. They spoke. They chanted.

Rich oral traditions the world over were in danger of being lost. The collection of hymns that formed the backbone of the Vedic religion had been passed on through generations in the Indo-Aryan language, for example. It couldn't be left to slip through the cracks or fade out slowly. It carried centuries of wisdom, heritage and tradition. If the language died, everything it carried would die with it. It had to be recorded.

The guardians of the Vedic traditions entrusted the learned and greatly respected grammarian Panini with the mission, believed to be in the fourth or fifth century BCE. Out of years of deep meditation came his work, *Ashtadhyayi*, a book of eight chapters, each further divided into quarters. An impressive classic of Sanskrit grammar and phonetics, it is summed up in almost 4,000 *sutras*. It survives in near-complete form till today. Panini didn't want it to be a rule book left to grow dusty in the vaults. He kept it brief, precise and pointed. Famed for its mathematical precision, it is a focused two-hour read, and read it should be. Panini understood another facet of language: it needs to be used, to be spoken, to be passed on. He recorded both forms—the language in sacred texts and the language spoken by the people. A language must live on.

THE FIRST DICTIONARIES

Across the speaking world, people felt the same: let's preserve our language and keep it safe somewhere. Let our great-grandchildren, centuries later, know how we spoke. These safe houses were dictionaries. So critical was the need to preserve language that even the cuneiform tablets in 2,000 BCE carried word lists, the first versions of a dictionary. A bilingual dictionary to boot, in Sumerian and Akkadian.

The first Sanskrit dictionary, more of a thesaurus, popularly called the *Amarakosha*, meaning everlasting treasure, was created by the scholar Amarasimha, one of the nine gems or *navratna* in the court of King Vikramaditya. He referred to eighteen earlier works, which haven't been found till now. But history may change yet. And the first English dictionary; who wrote that?

It may be the most spoken language in the world, but English wasn't spoken this way in earlier times, for sure.

'In þat lond ben trees þat beren wolle, as þogh it were of scheep.' Erm, translate that from English to English, please. Taken from a fourteenth-century work, *Mandeville's Travels*, this text is a filtered version of (an even older) Old English, which is a blend of Germanic, Old Norse and French.

Multiple attempts were made over the years to bring some sense and order into the many ways that many people spoke.

THE ENGLISH LANGUAGE NEEDS TO BEHAVE

'Discipline!' Samuel Johnson declared. Discipline is what the English language needed, and he set out on a heroic mission to give it just that.

He wasn't the first to attempt an English dictionary, of course. For a century and a half before him, word books of all kinds had been released. However, no one was satisfied. Surely, they were incomplete and inaccurate and could be improved upon? Perhaps a book to capture it all? A definitive and decisive text. Every word in the English language was hunted down, captured and nailed down into its correct position on the correct page. A group of London publishers got together and hired Samuel Johnson to create this word book.

Samuel Johnson set about 'fixing' English. Seven laborious years and six assistants later, in 1755 CE, he came up with *A Dictionary of the English Language*. Taking from medieval texts, using quotes and illustrations, Johnson herded together 40,000 words. It stacked up to almost a foot thick and weighed in at a bicep-building ten kilograms. This was no pocket dictionary.

Over the next many years, Johnson continued to fix the dictionary, finally declaring that 'fixing' a language was not feasible.

A language grows, morphs, loses and gains words. A language is alive.

A GIFT FROM A MURDERER

A century later, scholars regrouped and came to the same conclusion that they had 100 years ago. All the English dictionaries till then were once again incomplete, inaccurate and could surely be improved upon.

In 1879, Dr James Murray was given the task by the Oxford University Press. In today's lingo, Murray 'crowd-sourced'. He invited the public to send in words. The more, the merrier.

Here is where the tale gets macabre. The most words came in, almost twenty a day, from Dr William Minor. Excellent contributions, almost all of which got absorbed straight into the dictionary.

There was just one shocking revelation.

Dr Minor was a convicted murderer. A brilliant surgeon who fell prey to mental illness, he shot and killed a man, when in a state of paranoia. Locked in the Broadmoor Asylum for the criminally insane, Dr Minor sent in roughly 10,000 words, making him the biggest public contributor to the Oxford English Dictionary published soon after.

WORDS PINGING ACROSS THE WORLD

No longer kept under lock and key by wise old wordsmiths, words have escaped. Words in different languages are now captured in open dictionaries online—uncensored, unchecked, open to slang, jargon and experimental new entries being added. These are being added at an ever-increasing pace.

Every year, around 1,000 new words are added to an English Dictionary. Aiyyo! And yes, that's legit one of the latest additions to the Oxford Dictionary. At the other end of the spectrum is a language which prides itself on having the least number of words. Toki Pona is a language invented by Sonia Lang with only 137 words, which takes a mere two days to learn, and calls itself 'the language of good'.

EGLAF

Eglaf. What's that? Is that a word? Most dictionaries don't have it. The Urban Dictionary does. Eglaf claims to be a word that has no meaning. It can be used instead of any other word—sort of like stem cells.

I don't eglaf that anyone eglaf what eglaf really is.

A Ghost in the Pages

Dord!

Dord who? You talking to me?

You dord yourself!

Dord slipped into the Merriam-Webster dictionary unnoticed in 1934. No matter how well-checked, a ghost word, a complete fake, ends up in there. 'D or d' the hand-written word card said, 'is used for density'. 'D or d' merged into 'Dord' and sat unnoticed for five whole years, observing the world go by. At other times, however, the dictionary team uses fake words to weed out illegal copies of their dictionary. They throw in a rubbish word and soon enough, it appears somewhere online, copied exactly. Aha! Caught you, Dord!

But you can't sit and read a dictionary. You love stories. Whom do you have to thank for the first storytelling?

The Story of Stories

Let's do a quick check.

A) From time immemorial, stories were passed down generations, in songs. The rhyming structure helped people memorize them.

B)

The stories of old
Were sung, not told.
To last over time,
They were sung in rhyme.

If asked to, could you recite A or B? No looking back at them. They're both of exactly the same length, using the same number of words.

The average person (yes, yes, you don't like being called average!) remembers it in rhyme. And so, the wise old women (why should men always get the credit?) decided to pass stories down through their children and grandchildren in rhyme. We will exclude religious and spiritual texts from this list and stick to plain stories for now. Stories with no other purpose in life except being stories. Hmm . . . is that even possible?

The Mesopotamian godman: One of the earliest stories discovered was the Epic of Gilgamesh, written and rewritten by the Sumerians and the Babylonians over several centuries, in rhyme, on clay tablets. Gilgamesh went on a quest, chock-full of monsters and adventures, for immortality. He did find the immortality plant, but a serpent devoured it, presumably leaving the serpent immortal instead. And Gilgamesh? Later poems are found with varying conclusions, so we'll never know. Gilgamesh did achieve immortality in a way because he lives on and on in history.

The Egyptian sailor: In ancient Egypt, only religious tales were deemed worthy of being written in verse; stories were written in prose. The Egyptians had already graduated from clay to papyrus by the time one of the oldest Egyptian stories was written in 2,000 BCE. *The Shipwrecked Sailors* tells of the adventurous voyage of a man who landed in the fantastic Land of Punt yet had his heart set on getting back to Egypt. There's no place like home. Oh yes, he met a serpent, too. The Lord of Punt. This one talked, and quite a bit at that.

P.S. He didn't die in the end.

63

The Indian princely secrets: In India, some stories from ancient times are still so popular that there's no way you could get through your childhood without reading them, like the Jataka tales written originally in Pali and the famous *Panchatantra* written by Vishnusharma, with their much-adored talking animals.

Written across five books, the Panchatantra (that literally means the five secrets) stories from the third century BCE were meant to teach the three princes of the kingdom of Mahilaranya the ways of the world—about friendship, war, peace, loss and gain. These were weighty teachings, best taught through stories. Take, for example, *Mitrabheda*, the book that is an unforgettable lesson on friendship and how easy it is for outsiders to break it up. The lion king and bull were fast friends, but the two cunning jackals managed to turn them against each other. This resulted in the lion and bull hurling themselves into a furious battle . . . read the story yourself; no spoilers here, except that fighting with friends never ends well.

The Persian medicine: The Panchatantra travelled the world. Though the name means the five secrets, the tales inside these books turned out to be just the opposite—widely read by millions of children whom they enthralled forever.

The storytelling jackals, Damanaka and Karataka, first wandered off to Persia in the sixth century. King Khusrau of Persia had sent his court physician, Borzau, to India to bring back medicinal herbs. The physician fell under the storytelling spell of the brilliant jackals and decided that they needed to be introduced to the folks back home. He brought the Panchatantra back to Persia and translated it into Pahlavi as *Karirak ud Damanak*, after the jackals.

The book of five secrets was translated into Arabic in the eighth century, then into Latin, Hebrew, Greek, English . . . at current count, it's been translated into fifty languages.

The Greek fox: Greece saw its own animal fables emerge somewhere around 500 BCE as the wildly popular Aesop's Fables.

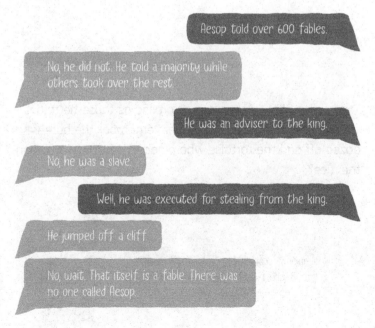

Aesop told over 600 fables.

No, he did not. He told a majority while others took over the rest.

He was an adviser to the king.

No, he was a slave.

Well, he was executed for stealing from the king.

He jumped off a cliff.

No, wait. That itself is a fable. There was no one called Aesop.

There was. Look him up, and you will find a curly-haired man.

That's what all Greek statues look like.

There unquestionably was an Aesop.

Not one ... many. Many storytellers made use of his name.

That's only after he was executed.

But he was not. He was set free.

The stories about Aesop are as prolific as those he told. Of course, the fables live on and on. Remember the hare who dozed off and the tortoise who plodded on slowly and won the race?

All ancient stories—Norse, Hindu, Greek, Egyptian—are full of dogs. Let's tell some of those stories instead.

AND THE MORAL OF THE STORY IS . . .

Most of the ancient stories had a moral, it turns out. To tell people to stay good or else! To be a good friend, to have patience, to think before acting, to pay attention to older-and-wiser people, to not spend so much time on video games . . . (Just slipped that in to check if you're paying attention.)

How do humans tell stories?
How do we speak at all when animals can't?

HUMANS
WIRED TO
SPEAK

Three Challenges

1. You can't talk with your lips together . . . you're trying it out right now, aren't you?

2. Try saying something, anything, while breathing in. You can't, can you? You really can't. But why can't you? Try again. Heh. Don't worry. No one can. All speech happens while you're breathing out.

3. This you can do. Read this out loud. While you pronounce sounds, notice what's happening in your mouth. Your tongue is doing an elaborate dance, and it knows exactly which steps to take, how to twist and where to land for each sound. All the while, your lips open and close through some secret message. For consonants, your lips shut off the air, while for vowels, they let it out. They all coordinate perfectly—like tandem gymnasts—for you to say the simplest things. Your breathing, your tongue and your lips.

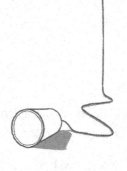

The Language Factory Inside

The larynx

The big language leap was actually a fall. The descended-larynx theory explains how, at some point along our evolutionary journey, our larynx dropped lower, which elongated our vocal tract, which in turn allowed humans to make sounds that animals couldn't.

Vocal cords vibrate at top speeds of over 100 vibrations per second, on average, while we're speaking. Children's vocal cords vibrate at around 300 vibrations per second. Of course, when we're angry or excited and hit the roof, the vibrations hit the roof, too. Men's vocal cords vibrate the slowest unless they're sports fans screaming when their team wins. Then their vocal cord vibrations rise to stratospheric levels.

The pharynx

The pharynx does its bit in providing the enclosed space needed for the production of sound.

Notice how when you've had a sudden shock or panic or are surprised, you can't speak? Someone may ask you, 'What's up? Cat* got your tongue?' or 'Swallowed your tongue?' Turns out that this shutting up has nothing to do with your tongue. It is the throat muscles that tighten in times of stress.

The cat has nothing to do with it either. The cat is being made a scapegoat. The idiom, 'cat got your tongue', has filtered down from old times of black cats and witches when the superstitious insisted on illogical reasons for everything.

The tongue

The tongue itself has a hero's role in speech production. Nothing to do with cats. Parrots, maybe. That's coming up.

The human tongue is as quick as a snake. It darts around, rolls, flips, twists and thwacks. It even extracts something stuck between your teeth, but that has nothing to do with language (neither has the cat, as I keep saying). The human tongue can enable more than ninety words per minute. Different languages demand different things from the tongue. I challenge any non-native speaker of Malayalam, for example, to say *kozhi* (chicken). I've tried often, and it has been thoroughly entertaining (to everyone but me). Ask a non-native speaker of French to roll their R's for *heureuse* (happy). Not very happy if you can't get it right. Your tongue rolls should get some eye-rolls.

Back to parrots, as I had promised. Parrots have thick tongues, which help them pronounce certain words by hitting their tongues against the insides of their mouths. Can they speak? Coming up, coming up . . . remember, curiosity killed the cat. (Though the cat still has nothing to do with any of this.)

The other factory workers

The lips, teeth, jaw, palate and nose, all work together to help you speak. Even while you're relaxing or singing something random while swinging in the park, your body's hard at work, making that song happen.

Wait—did I slip in the nose? Yes, the nose has a role in speech. Remember when you had that cold and your breathing got laboured and you went around saying, 'I god a bad gold'? Nasalized sounds are part of speech, common in French, such as *pain* (bread), and in Hindi, such as *kaanch* (glass) or *ma* (pronounced maa-nh, especially when you're complaining).

Language, as we know, isn't about you talking in a bubble in outer space with no one else around. It is communication.

It's about speaking, listening and understanding one another. Now, even more body parts join the party.

The ears receive the sounds that others make and send them on to your brain, which makes sense of these sounds. Your hands gesture, your body moves and your eyes receive signals, spot danger and make and read expressions. You know the difference between when you mother's saying, 'What's this?' and her face tells you she's curious (no mention of cats anymore). And when she's saying, 'What's this?', and you've got to dive for cover. Of course, other things help in communication, like, in the second scenario, the pieces of the broken vase which she blames on your cricket ball, and you blame it on the cat.

What's missing?

In 2016, scientist Fitch and his team declared that the vocal cords of a certain individual were speech-ready. Here's the thing. The individual was a monkey, a macaque. Monkeys and apes, most scientists agree, make a whole range of sounds. They could have spoken, but they don't. So, what's missing?

The processor—the CPU, the controller, the master—is the brain. The brain needs to interpret sounds and send out messages to respond. The brain-vocal cord connection in animals isn't yet at the stage it's got to in humans.

THE BRAIN: 'THIS IS YOUR CAPTAIN SPEAKING.'

The brain must receive signals, make sense of them, then check thoughts for a response, put these thoughts into language, form words, and then get the factory workers to output those words. All in a fraction of a second.

The brain is nowhere near being understood completely, but these are some of the parts of the brain identified in language.

Wernicke's Area is tasked with understanding and interpreting language.

Broca's Area helps express your thoughts in words.

The Motor Cortex helps your vocal apparatus translate signals from Broca's Area. (Now that you've thought it, go on and say it.)

Arcuate Fasciculus is a bundle of nerves connecting the Broca's and Wernicke's areas so that you can understand and speak. That's also what you hear someone say just before they go on to the stage, 'I'm a bundle of nerves'. Next time, tell them to say, 'I'm an Arcuate Fasciculus'. Ironically, it is because of serious injuries to certain parts of the brain that their role in language was understood.

Have you noticed that it's only when something goes away that you miss it?

The One-Word Man: Broca's Area

'Tan,' he said. And they gave him water. 'Tan,' he said, because the water was too cold. 'Tan,' he said when the water was too hot. 'Tan' is all he ever said. Sometimes, he said, 'Tan Tan.'

They called him Tan, but his real name was Louis Victor Leborgne. One day, in 1861, the 30-year-old was checked into a Paris hospital because he had begun to utter just that one word.

Doctor Pierre Paul Broca noticed that the patient could count, tell time, and was generally aware of things. He just couldn't speak. After Tan passed on, a large lesion was found in the frontal lobe of his brain.

Later named Broca's Area, it is part of a complex network that orders information in our brains and sends out messages about what we have to say, even before we say it. And we know about it now, thanks to that unforgettable one-word man.

Word Salads:
Wernicke's Area

In the flurry of excitement after Paul Broca's discoveries, the neurology world went into further huddles and debates and studies and experiments and theories.

In 1874, Carl Wernicke, a German neurologist, noticed that his patients were the opposite of Broca's. Wernicke found that his patients could speak but they could neither understand nor make themselves understood. They formed words and sentences that made no sense—basically word salads.

Wernicke's Area came to be known as the area in the brain accountable for receiving and understanding language.

HOW THEY FOUND THE FOX

Remember the FOXP2 gene? Its mutation in humans made it possible for us to speak. Or at least one of the things that made it possible for us to speak. This gene, too, was identified through people in whom the gene was malfunctioning. Fifteen members of a large family over three generations had problems with language, and these people were diagnosed with problems in their FOXP2.

We've just scratched the surface, of course. Many parts of the brain connect in the understanding, processing and delivery of language. We've got some mega factories inside us. It's going to be a long time before we understand them ourselves.

Dogs have 500 million neurons in our brains, double that of cats. I hope that finally settles the debate of who is smarter.

Bird Brain!

The human brain is packed with 86,000,000,000 neurons. Just to put that into perspective, the pigeon's is estimated at 300,000,000. Bird brain, really? The mosquito's brain is estimated to have only 220,000 neurons, and it still manages to outfox me.

GROW YOUR OWN BRAIN

To toss all our calculations out of whack, our brains can grow new neural connections. In an experiment, after six months of being taught to read, children had not only grown their vocabularies but also made new white matter connections in their brains.

That's exactly why the doctor advises the elderly to do puzzles or crosswords, or why you should try learning new things or new languages (or reading this book). You can grow your own brain.

But why can't animals talk?
Or can they?

NON-HUMAN LANGUAGE

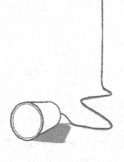

My Dog Started Off
This Book

A few years back, I was walking my dog, Marcopolo.

'Look,' I told him sternly. 'This isn't going to be a long, rambling walk. I've got way too much work waiting.'

He cocked his head at me and whined.

'Cry all you want, but we've got to go home, so hurry up and do your thing,' I said.

He didn't. He didn't hurry, and he didn't do his thing. He, most stubbornly, took half an hour longer. Then, finally, when we were on our way back home, he began to bark hysterically and pull on his leash, steering us towards a tree. It took all my strength to keep him (and me, on the end of that leash) from jumping up that tree.

'Look!' said his barks. 'A squirrel. You've got to let me chase the squirrel. You can't say no.'

'No!' I said. 'We are going back home. Bad dog!'

Like all dog owners, I am convinced Marcopolo understood every word I said. The way I understood his barking. Scientists, however, disagree. Dogs can be taught to understand about 100 words on average, apparently. So, Marcopolo would have only got (from all that I had said): 'walk', 'wait', 'home', 'hurry', 'bad', 'dog' and 'no'. Confusing!

'Don't worry, Marco,' I told him, 'I know you're much smarter than the average dog.'

'Or the average human,' he barked back.

At least, I'm convinced he did.

That's where the idea for this book came to me. From my dog. Can animals understand our language? Can they communicate in their own? How did we end up being the only talking animals around? There's so much about language that's mysterious, and that's when I began to delve into it—a little further each day.

This book was written by Jane. And me. And not by a chatbot.

Do animals have languages that humans just can't understand?

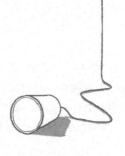

Let's Keep
This Secret

Marcopolo would sniff every single tree and every single lamppost on our walks.

'Oh, come on, Marco,' I'd say. 'Every lamppost smells the same, and how different can it be from morning to afternoon?'

I was wrong on both counts.

Marcopolo was decoding information left by other dogs. One whiff told him which dogs had peed there, their gender, age, hierarchy in a pack and lots more that he won't tell me. Rhinos get that from dung. Okay, time to stop this train of thought.

In short, animals communicate. We know that. Anyone who's walked under the wide canopy of a large tree at dusk will have heard birds chirping and twittering and creating a huge ruckus. It's not for nothing that they call it a parliament of owls or an unkindness of ravens or a murder of crows, as if crows were plotting whom to murder from up there. Just goes to show that humans really don't understand animal language. Perhaps animals prefer it that way—keeping it secret from us.

LANGUAGES THAT NEED NO WORDS

Animals can warn, threaten, court, attract, inform or challenge each other without a single word. Their communication is through signals that are visual, physical, auditory and even chemical and electric.

Here is a list of some of the weird communication channels used and what they mean (as if murders and dung aren't weird enough):

A spider's web vibrating: I know who's coming for dinner or who's coming as dinner. Friend, foe, prey . . .

Honeybee dance: Touch me and find out where I found the honey and how to get there without Google Maps.

Greengrocer cicadas clenching their abdomens: Not a tummy pain. Just to make a noise loud enough to deafen ourselves.

Male green anole lizard flapping its neck: This is my home. Get out!

Silverback gorilla thumping his chest: This is my home. Get out!

Australian lizard tail-flicking: This is my home. Get out! A whole lot of animals tell us this, so we really need to get out of their home spaces and not construct our buildings all over them.

Kākāpō parrot: I almost went extinct, so my whole gang and I are going to sing so loud that we'll make sure you never let that happen to us again.

Electric fish sending out weak electric signals: Come, meet me, and let's send out weak electric signals together. (Two fish can tune their wavelengths to produce the same voltage.)

Moth secreting pheromones: Come, meet me.

Ant secreting pheromones: Danger! Or Food! Or Both!

Human spotting ant or moth: Eeeeeks!

Elephant emitting infrasound: Hey, this is an elephant 170 miles away. Can you hear me? At twenty hertz, this is too low for any human to hear, so let's gossip about them.

Goodbye in Elephantese

In 2012, Lawrence Anthony, a passionate conservationist, passed away in his house in KwaZulu-Natal, South Africa. From twelve miles away, two herds of wild elephants began moving towards his house. They lumbered over and silently stood outside. After two days, they walked away. These were wild elephants Anthony had rescued earlier. No one had informed or called them. They seemed to know how to communicate this to one another, and turned up for a last goodbye. How? Perhaps humans have a long way to go in understanding that there's much more to communication than we can fathom.

Could animals be trained to understand human language?

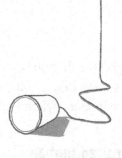

Animals Raised as Humans

ANIMAL BRAINS LOOK JUST LIKE OURS

Animal brains look like ours externally. The chimpanzee shares 98% of our DNA, though our brains are thrice as large. (We're larger, too, so there's that.) But you don't hear of a chimp with a 40,000-word vocabulary. Why not?

In an attempt to understand why not, researchers recorded monkey chatter. From a study of the vervet monkeys in Africa, researchers learnt that on spotting predators, they called out. Fascinatingly, these calls weren't the same. They communicated exactly which predator lurked and what the others should do. The leopard alarm call meant: *scamper up the tree*. The eagle alarm meant: *not too high on the tree. Angry bird approaching*. The snake alarm meant: *tree or no tree. Just freeze*. Still, it was not speech.

Could animals be taught human language? Certainly not if they were only surrounded by other animals. But could a chimp learn human language if brought up with humans?

Nim Chimpsky: raised human

In 1973, a Columbia University professor, Herbert Terrace, kept a baby chimpanzee with a foster family. He attempted to teach the baby sign language, surrounded by humans. Nim Chimpsky (named after the linguist Noam Chomsky) learnt about 125 signs by the time he was shifted to another house because he was too boisterous with the human kids. (He was just being a chimp.)

Later, Nim was sent to live in a cage in a lab with other chimps. There was no proof that he was using language, and so the research project was halted, and there was no more use for Nim. His friends finally stepped in to save him from a medical lab, and he got to live out the rest of his life in an animal sanctuary. Whenever any of his old human friends from Project Nim visited, he would eagerly break into sign language with them.

It was finally agreed upon that Nim was as much a human as any of us are chimps.

'Take the vacuum cleaner outside, Kanzi.'

Sue Savage-Rumbaugh worked with Kanzi, the bonobo, in her surroundings inhabited by both humans and bonobos.

Kanzi was taught to click certain keys on a specially made keyboard with symbols to communicate what he wanted. He soon learnt to hit the correct symbols, with a vocabulary of many hundred symbols and understood a bit of spoken English too. For example, 'Take the vacuum cleaner outside, Kanzi.' Why the outside needed vacuuming was something Kanzi (or I) couldn't comprehend. Was he using language? No.

Service dogs are trained to alert hearing-impaired humans to alarms, phones, doorbells, thunder, babies' cries, etc. Or to the oven pinging that the cake is ready.

If animals can't talk humanese, can humans learn animalese?

The Life-Saving Song

Male whales sing. All males sing the same song and change it every year. By magic, mystery or master communication, once a song changes, they all begin to sing the new song within a week. People love whale songs, which win awards and get the most likes, and all that. But what do whales care? They have no walls or showcases to put prizes on. Nor cameras to click selfies with. But their singing actually saved them once upon a time.

This singing is made by what? A fish?

Well, technically it's a mammal.

That's beautiful. Someday, I'll take my grandkids to hear it.

Not likely. The whales may not last till then, at the rate they're being hunted.

We can't let that happen. Let's raise our own voices.

Not as melodious as the whales, but yeah, we can.

Wide protests by people who realized that these beautiful, talented beings were being hunted to extinction triggered a UN ban on whaling for ten years. The whales actually saved themselves by singing.

Though we love the music, whales aren't really entertaining each other on their long, long swims across wide, wide oceans. They use their calls for echolocation to communicate with one another and navigate their way through the echoes of their calls bouncing off the shores. Beluga whales are such expert navigators that they can size up an object behind an opaque surface, which human technology has been struggling to do for years.

Humans realized quickly that we could use animal communication for our own purposes. There are, for example, quite a few projects where defence forces work with dolphins to catch enemy submarines or locate buried mines. We may not speak animal languages, but we can still use them.

Listen to Your Dog

The catastrophic tsunami of 2004, which left thousands of people dead, killed no free animals. Days, hours, minutes before the thirty-foot waves from the tsunami hit the shore, the animals had already escaped to higher ground. Across India, Thailand, Indonesia and Sri Lanka. The only animals killed were the chained ones—pets or cattle. In fact, elephants in Khao Lak in Thailand broke their chains and carried themselves and their surprised handlers to higher ground. Humans who had run along with their animals survived.

More astonishing is that animals can pick up tremors a week before a tsunami hits, which the most advanced technology and seismic sensors can't.

It isn't that only our modern animals are exceptionally clever. Historian Thucydides recorded seeing hordes of animals fleeing the city of Helice many days before the mega earthquake of 373 BCE hit.

If you need further convincing, ask how birds never fly into storms. And if your dog begins to bark manically, don't hush him; just listen. His barking could save your life. Or, of course, it could be because of the cat next door.

It's funny how we much we want animals to talk our language, isn't it?

Barking Up the Wrong Tree

While we can't prove that animals talk, we can't have enough of talking animals. Right from the *Panchatantra* and Aesop's Fables down the ages to the PAW Patrol series.

Anthropomorphism. We delight in giving animals human words or behaviour. You've heard someone laughing like a hyena? Hyenas don't laugh. That shrill sound is caused by stress.

A bit of a laugh about how some idioms came to be (and came to be wrong, of course):

These are howlers. Humanese is a hilarious language.

1. Straight from the horse's mouth

This is supposed to tell you that the message came directly from the source. What, a neigh? This idiom is lifted off the horse race-betting world. The jockeys, trainers and grooms who tended to the horse and were closest to it leaked tips and secrets.

2. A little bird told me

You blame it on the little bird when you don't want to divulge your secret source. Birds, like horses (of course), don't tell secrets or much else. They can't speak. The phrase comes from a biblical line: 'for a bird of the air shall carry the voice' and has been claiming to reveal secrets ever since.

3. Kangaroo court

Kangaroos clearly don't hold court; like owls don't have parliaments. A kangaroo court refers to a hastily put-together clutch of people whose judgement you refuse to accept. Taken from the time when ineffective judges hopped around like kangaroos, proclaiming judgement on one case after the other, packing in so many in a day that they couldn't do any real justice.

4. Swan song

A last huge achievement before anyone retires or leaves. It is supposed to refer to the last beautiful song a swan sings before it dies. The problem? A swan doesn't sing before it dies. The idiom, nevertheless, lives on.

5. Scapegoat

When you're blamed for something that's not your fault, you can blame this Hebrew tradition. Before the holy day of Yom Kippur, a goat would be turned out into the wilderness. The community would symbolically place all their sins on the head of this innocent goat and then turn it out. Silly goats! The people, not the scapegoat.

6. Crocodile tears

'You're shedding fake tears. We don't believe you—those are crocodile tears.' Your tears may be real enough, but a crocodile doesn't shed tears, which is why they're fake.

7. Cock-and-bull story

A totally unbelievable tale, all made-up, no truth. However, unless their vocal cords have changed dramatically over the centuries, cocks and bulls don't go around storytelling. One root of this phrase is traced back to two inns on the outskirts of London, one called The Cock and the other, The Bull. As people went from one to the other, retelling stories they'd heard while getting drunker, the stories grew wilder and more fantastical. But there may be no truth to this version either. Do you think this itself is a cock-and-bull story?

So many experiments on animals and language. And how about us humans?

EXPERIMENTS AND RECORDS

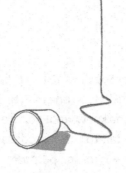

The Forbidden Experiments

We aren't the only . . . ahem, intelligent, curious people interested in finding out more about language. Throughout history, there were thousands who were eager to crack the mystery of our talking. Let's talk a bit about the early illogical, cruel experiments here because it's as important to know what we shouldn't do as it is to know what we could.

The thing about kings

Kings are a good place to start. Kings and their reigns and rulings, their kingdoms and queens, and their battles and beards. Everything about kings was dutifully recorded.

The other thing about kings, especially those in earlier eras was that they thought they were the cat's whiskers, the bee's knees, the unicorn's horn, i.e., the most important people ever. They felt invincible, perhaps even immortal, direct descendants of gods.

Kings often believed that the preposterous things they did benefited mankind. No one in their courts dared tell them otherwise. Everyone knew what going against the bee's knees meant. You were fed to the crocodiles or lions or whichever animal that king kept for the purpose.

Though many kings were kind and benevolent, the alarming bits about them also need to go down alongside their names. History needs to be objective.

Language deprivation experiments, often referred to as forbidden experiments, were ones in which children were deprived of ever listening to or learning a language, presumably to see what language they began to speak naturally.

Becos, just becos

Whose culture was the first, the oldest and the original? The Egyptians or the Phrygians?

The argument raged over the centuries and across dynasties. Then, Egyptian Pharaoh Psamtik I decided to settle this debate once and for all. Not by flipping a coin, no. The Pharaoh chose two very young children, who hadn't yet begun to babble, and put them into the care of a herdsman who was given strict instructions on how to raise them.

They were to be kept isolated in a cottage by themselves, with all their needs taken care of. There was to be no human contact. Goats were let in occasionally so that the children could have milk. They were to hear no words—none whatsoever. The royal goal was to find out which language they spoke first. Surely, if these tiny humans, in these conditions, spoke a language, that ought to be the first language ever spoken by any human. (No, don't ask me about the logic—it wasn't my experiment.)

The herdsman, like every other subject, followed the king's word to a T, and spoke no word to the toddlers. Two years later, he opened the door. The children ran to him, shouting out, 'Becos'. When the herdsman presented them to the king, the toddlers once again said, 'Becos'. They had a clear winner. 'Becos' was the Phyrgian word for bread.

No coos, no cuddles

Frederick II, the eighteenth-century King of Prussia, spoke many languages fluently and was obsessed with finding the first language too.

His experiment saw babies taken from their mothers to be brought up by nurses, who were supposed to feed and clean them but never speak to them. No coos or cuddles. No signs of love or care, and no speech at all. In one of the ghastliest and saddest outcomes of these forbidden experiments, it is said that none of the babies spoke, but worse, none of them survived.

The island of no escape

King James IV of Scotland was fascinated with languages and could understand quite a few, but he wanted to go further—to uncover what god's own language was.

In 1493 CE, he had a mute woman and two children isolated on the desolate island of Inchkeith. After recording the story faithfully till this point, history loses its ending. You know how it is when you're reading a book, turning page after page with bated breath, and then you get to the last page to find it's been torn out? It's the same here. There is no agreement on how this experiment ended.

The house of silence

Akbar the Great decided to test his own theory of language in the late sixteenth century. Speaking a language, he said, was the result of hearing spoken language. If not heard, it could not be spoken. Abul Fazl, Akbar's court historian, was the first to record the experiment in the *Akbarnama*.

Emperor Akbar had a group of young children isolated in the care of nurses in a place that would come to be called the Dumb House. The nurses were not to speak to the babies.

Four years later, the emperor himself came to visit the children, and none of them could really speak coherently at that point, beyond making undecipherable noises.

In his early-eighteenth-century writing on the history of the Mughal Empire, French historian Francois Catrou offers a happier ending to this story. Catrou says that Akbar found the children not speaking the 'original' language or any other language but communicating in sign language. After all, their nurses were prohibited from speaking to them, but not signing with them.

**Do language experiments still exist,
or did they die out with the medieval kings?**

From
Island to Lab

Fast forward to our times. The language deprivation experiments died out. Phew! But language experiments didn't.

Most major universities today offer departments and advanced degrees in linguistics. Testing is now strictly controlled under the most ethical standards.

Here are some eye-openers achieved via MRIs or brain scans, for example, used to note which areas of the brain light up when active.

The brain works less when you know more

An experiment by the University of Tokyo found that first-time learners of Japanese showed more brain activity when they began to study the language, which slowed down when they got better at it. Sort of like how you take cycling for granted when you know how to do it. You don't really need to think about your legs pedalling.

You know your mother tongue even if you don't know that you know it

In an experiment conducted at McGill University in Canada, scientists showed that the brain remembers your first language, even if you consciously don't. It gets hardwired into your brain. Studies on children who had stopped speaking their native languages as toddlers (and were adopted into families which didn't speak the native language) didn't show signs of understanding it later, but their brains lit up when they heard it.

The brain learns language even when its language-learning centre is damaged

A study done at Georgetown University in the USA showed that infants who had strokes damaging the language areas in the left hemisphere of their brains had the right hemisphere take on those roles.

Moving beyond those who could speak no language to . . . how many languages do you speak?

Here Come the Polyglots

If you can speak two languages, you're bilingual.

More than two? Multilingual.

If you can manage five languages fluently, you get the right to call yourself a polyglot.

Ten languages earn you the hyperpolyglot label.

The 2011 census showed that half the Indian population aged 20–24 is bilingual. Youngsters are picking up more languages quickly. Since many of us in India speak more than one language already, we've only got to pick up a few more to join the club of these world-famous polyglots.

Cleopatra: a tongue with many strings

The beautiful and ambitious Queen of the Nile got her siblings killed so that she could claim the throne, then ruled for twenty-one years, by whatever means it took, in Egypt in the first century BCE. She even controlled how she died, which was by her own hand when she was thirty-nine years old.

Getting the throne is one thing but staying on it that long is quite another. A brilliant strategist, she made sure she was fluent in nine languages, at least to talk to her subjects. Plutarch, the historian, said of her, 'Her tongue was like an instrument of many strings, she could readily turn to whatever language she pleased . . . she very seldom had the need of an interpreter.'

Mithridates VI: a new word and a new poison every day

Mithridates VI of Pontus (a place now in Turkey) had two unique survival skills. The first skill involved poisoning himself every day. Survival by poisoning? Mithridates wanted to strengthen himself so that no poison would strike him dead, so he popped a bit daily to get used to it.

His second skill was language. The historian, Pliny the Elder, spoke of Mithridates as '. . . king of twenty-two nations, administered their laws in many languages, and could harangue in all of them, without employing an interpreter.' And as we all know, haranguing or harassing someone in their language takes the most skill.

Kavi Yogi Maharishi Dr Shuddhananda Bharati: 250 books in five languages

Kavi Yogi Shuddhananda Bharati was a playwright, poet, essayist, lyricist, translator and yogi in the early 1900s. He wasn't just a regular writer but an award-winning one. He has over 250 published works to his credit. His body of work spans languages: 173 in Tamil, four in Hindi, three in Telegu, fifty in English and six in French. Besides original works, he translated several classics from other languages into Tamil.

Here is one last badge for Dr Shuddhananda Bharati. He wrote his ultimate work, *Bharata Shakti*, which won the highest Tamil literary prize, while in silent meditation for twenty-five years.

Emil Krebs: a hundred languages and counting

Emil Krebs was allegedly a master of sixty-eight languages.

Wait, it's not over yet. He knew 111 more!

Emil started early, roaming around and muttering to himself as a young lad. Nowadays, in the age of cell phones, it's a common sight, but that wasn't the case in the late 1800s. Emil Krebs was teaching himself languages and was quickly picked up by the German army as an interpreter and sent to China. He spent most of his nights studying even more languages—Manchurian, Mongolian, Tibetan—while the world went to war. Every day, he turned to a different language. Turkish Tuesdays weren't just a restaurant special for Krebs.

Emil Kerb's brain has been preserved for research. Perhaps, one day, its mysteries will be unlocked.

Noah Webster: twenty-six languages needed for the job

The man who introduced us to 70,000 words, their spellings, origin and pronunciations. Noah Webster began his dictionary in the 1700s and ended it in the 1800s. To know where words came from, Webster taught himself twenty-six languages.

Noah Webster was determined to give his country, America, its own word culture. So, he added American words to the existing British ones in the English dictionaries. Native American foods and clothing got their mention, like moccasin, for one. (Or two, because what would you do with one moccasin?) And so did skunk. Let me show you how it's spelt, Noah demonstrated, if not how it smelled.

Jean-Francois Champollion: the hieroglyphics code cracker

It was the beginning of the 1800s. Napoleon Bonaparte's army had just discovered a black stone in Egypt, unlike any other black stone. All right, it was unlike any stone ever found.

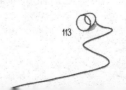

The Rosetta Stone had inscriptions in Greek, Egyptian Demotic and hieroglyphics.

Scholars were hitting their heads against a (stone) wall, though many had almost-there success. Champollion, who had been demonstrating his magical language skills since childhood, offered his own solution. Later, he went to Egypt to the Valley of the Kings and decoded further secrets that had been buried for 2,000 years, earning him the moniker of the Founding Father of Egyptology.

HOW DO YOU KNOW YOU'RE FLUENT?

There are many polyglots claiming that they can speak several languages.

You could chat with your bus driver in his language, demand what you want from the sweet seller in theirs, pass your school exams in your first, second and third languages and trade impolite words with your friend in his language. That's a little bit in a lot of languages, right? Even your dog has, like the average dog, about a 100-word vocabulary in human language. So, how many words are enough? Is there a grid to specify the point at which one is fluent?

There are, of course, scales to measure language fluency (the CEFR Global Scale is one), and regrettably, neither your dog nor mine will make it.

This is roughly how your language learning journey goes: It is said that a baby learns the melody of its mother tongue even before being born. Teenagers have a vocabulary of around 20,000 words and adults average 40,000 words. Graduates and post-graduates (and voracious readers, of course) could double that.

The Secret Agents in this Book

A good way to increase your vocabulary is to tag any word you don't know in a book you're reading and look up its meaning.

Writers of children's books are supposed to make the words simple. Many of us are stubborn and don't.

Instead of lazy words like 'nice' or 'great', you will, hopefully, find more nuanced ones that will challenge you and make you a little wiser on the last page than you were on the first. Any idea how many new words or phrases you've added to your vocabulary through this book? (Snuck a couple into this paragraph already.)

While everyone has been learning new words, who's been creating them?

DIFFERENCES ACROSS THE WORLD

Where Do New Words Come from?

When Samuel Johnson composed his dictionary, he noted that there were no words starting with X. Today, the Oxford English Dictionary has over 300 entries. Where were all these words hiding? Where do new words come from?

Pick up the shiny things

Languages act like birds sometimes. A crow brings gifts of shiny trinkets to houses it likes (stolen from houses it doesn't like, maybe). Similarly, many words have just hopped around the world, from one language to another. That's why many words sound similar in several languages which are far apart globally.

English has words creeping in from hundreds of different languages, ancient and new, and there will be still newer ones that will be added before this book goes to print.

'Surprise', for example, is said to come from 'taken hold of' in French, Latin and even, weirdly enough, from 'fancy dish'. Not sure where that came from, but it sure is a surprise.

Pop and sizzle

Sounds of words are formally accepted as their official names. Buzz, hiss, crash, squeak . . .

1+1+1+

Sanskrit and German, and all languages that compound words, keep clubbing them together to form new ones.

'Could you put on your "hand-shoe" before you go out into the cold? Or you'll end up in the "sick-house".' In German, that's *handschuh* and *krankhaus* for you. Not what they taught you in the garden for children—kindergarten?

Slice it up

The opposite of adding on word after word is cutting a word short and then managing to get your shorter version into the dictionary, like 'gym', 'flu' and even 'phone'. Would you hear anyone nowadays say they're using the telephone to inform the gymnasium that they will be missing a session because of influenza?

Sometimes, you'd never guess the original version of a shortened word. 'Taximeter cabriolet'? Both the words taxi and cab come from there.

I'll use your name

Eponyms are words that come from the names of people or companies or places. The way we 'xerox' something while downing a 'coke' or a 'sandwich'. You're going to 'Google' this, aren't you?

Hooligan was the name of a rowdy Irish family. Panic was set off when the Greek God Pan created nameless terror, while the much more helpful Greek God Atlas held up the heavens and gave us the name of the book of world maps.

Fictional characters have also donated words. Scrooge is the heartless moneylender who overworked and underpaid people in *A Christmas Carol* by Charles Dickens. You don't need to be an 'Einstein' to know that someone who is miserly deserves to be called a 'Scrooge'. And if you happen to wear *jodhpuris* or *kolhapuris*, you'll know that places, too, lend themselves to words.

ROFLACND.
Rolling On Floor Laughing
At Cat Next Door.

Only letters, please

LOL, TTYL, G2G, BRB, IDK . . . or maybe not, because you're likely to know what these recent acronyms stand for. Often, the older acronyms have got so settled in that we stop thinking about the original words that spell out the acronym. Each gets its own pronunciation and just becomes a word instead of a series of words.

Why does GOAT get to be
God Of All Things? Unfair!

What's the Full Form of . . .

It's likely you use all these words. It's equally likely that you've forgotten their full forms. Try guessing their full forms before you get to the key.

1. SCUBA
2. SIM
3. cc
4. CAT scan
5. RADAR

6. ISRO
7. PAN
8. GIF
9. MODEM
10. LASER

Answer key

1. Self-contained Underwater Breathing Apparatus
2. Subscriber Identification Module
3. Carbon Copy
4. Computerized Axial Tomography
5. Radio Detecting and Ranging

6. Indian Space Research Organisation
7. Permanent Account Number
8. Graphics Interchange Format
9. Modulator-Demodulator
10. Light Amplification by Stimulated Emission of Radiation

Can you guess where a word came from?
(Easier than you think it is.)

The Helpless-King Game

It's fun to trace the bloodline of a word, pick it out of its family tree and chuckle over some of the crazy twists it's had in its long life. This is called etymology. It is the study of where words come from, their origins traced to when they first popped up in history, and their journeys chronicled since then.

Here are some of my favourites, but I won't give them up easily. I'll give you the story, and you try to guess the word before you come to the end of the story and the answer.

The king is helpless

This word came from the Persian *shah mat*, which means the king is helpless. It's used in chess. If you play chess, it's the word that ends the game. Got it or given up? And you've got to give up if you're caught in a **checkmate**.

King Julien is a ghost

If you've seen the movie *Madagascar*, you'll get this at once. King Julien is a certain species of animal typical of Madagascar. The name of this species comes from the Latin word for ghosts you spot at night, *lemures*. These little ones do look strange, but definitely not scary-strange, more charming-strange, if you've actually seen a **lemur**.

It was first made with fish

Seafood sauce is *kecap ikan*, Worcestershire sauce is *kecap ingeriss*, soy sauce is *kecap bango*. You'll find these bottles on dining tables across Indonesia, Malaysia and Singapore. What do you think *kecap* is in English? Here's a further hint: The *kecap* of tomatoes arrived at the table the latest because tomatoes were considered poisonous for the longest time. Now, of course, you'd die without it, not with it. You can't get through your burger and fries without your **ketchup**.

Not enough salt

Food again? Not really. In the Roman Empire, salt was almost as precious as gold. Salt was needed to make food edible and for preservation. It became the much-prized and much-needed payment to labourers. The Latin word *sal* for salt donated the word we use thousands of years later for pay. Nothing as tasty as your first **salary**.

Gold grabbers

Speaking of actual gold, of which we had plenty in India, palanquins and wedding processions were easy targets for highwaymen who knew they would be laden with gold. This word comes from the Sanskrit *sthagati*, translated in this case to mean wait. As the people made their way across secluded lands from one state to another, these highwaymen thieves hid on the routes, waiting to descend on them and rob them blind. The **thugs**!

Save yourself from the beast

The Minotaur had King Theseus trapped in a gigantic labyrinth. Greek mythology's fierce monster with a man's body and a bull's head thought the king would perish in there. But the king had a human's brain, after all, while the Minotaur had that of a bull. King Theseus used a ball of yarn, also called a clew, to lay out his path so that he could solve the puzzle, and I'm not giving you another **clue**.

Beware of the evils of gambling

Al Zahr in thirteenth-century Arabic was an innocent enough word, and a fun one, too. It was the word used for dice. However, the dice were used in shady, sinister gambling games, which came with a risk. When the word, the dice and the games were brought back to England, they came with a warning. The same warning you're used to seeing now as a health or a fire or a lightning **hazard**.

Goat song

I am not kidding you. One of the origins this word traces back to is *tragos*, which means goat, and *oide*, which means ode. In ancient Greece, either in theatre or in mythology or songs or sacrifices, goats were not a very happy happening. What a **tragedy**!

Look out, there's a mouse inside you!

A word origin story so funny, it must be made up, surely. This word is now used to show off how strong you are. You know how you flex your biceps and triceps and all that? It is said to come from the Latin *mus*, meaning mouse. Sorry to disappoint you, but a mouse running under your skin looks like your **muscle**.

The word Dogma comes from latin and means a firm belief. Though I personally have a firm belief that it comes from 'dog'.

Covid's favourite word

A word being tossed around all through the pandemic, this one. It came from the fourteenth-century Black Death, the plague which killed thousands of people. Therefore, ships were ordered to dock out of land in isolation, not have travellers or sailors mingling or spreading it to anyone on the mainland. Stay out there for forty days, or how you'd say it in Italian: '*quaranta giorni*'. Now, it's down to a week, or even four days, your period of **quarantine**.

> **Words are also born and raised in a region, like plants or animals indigenous to that region. Erm . . . what?**

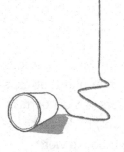

Fire Energy

You're invited to a world tour of weddings and stomach aches now—one not leading to the other, hopefully. It is intriguing to understand how and why words spring up in a culture. You can't have just any kind of stomach ache or any kind of wedding in any culture.

Watch while the doctor taps the elderly woman's stomach. 'You're absolutely okay,' he says.

She shakes her head miserably. 'I have no appetite. I can feel a huge lump in my stomach.'

'The scans are normal. Your blood reports are normal,' the doctor says in his kindest bedside manner.

'It is the "fire energy",' the woman declares. 'You foreign doctors don't know how to treat it.'

Hwa Byung is a complaint that the stomach holds on to anger (*Hwa* or fire) and that causes the illness (*Byung*). Obviously, to doctors in most parts of the world, this means nothing. It would only make sense in Korean culture and is a sample of a culture-bound word.

A culture of stomach aches? Could stomachs differ so much across countries?

The Mayans of Mexico named eight kinds of diarrhoea. No one medicine could cure all eight.

In France, a patient may complain of stomach pain because of *crise de foie*, a condition specific to eating too much fatty liver, perhaps?

In Hindi, you could complain of *choohe kudna*, the sensation of rats jumping inside you. That's your tummy crying out from hunger. (Even though your mother says you've eaten an hour earlier.)

In South America, you'd blame it on spirits leaving your body. That, quite obviously, is the reason behind your lack of appetite and pain. *Susto* is how you'd explain that your spirit has been snatched away, leaving you listless? (*Sust* in Hindi, how coincidental is that?)

No antacids will do, doctor, the spirit needs to be chased, caught, captured and returned or this patient will never eat again.

If you have to go up in front of a group and explain stomach aches, you'd probably have butterflies in your stomach, which is that strange fluttering feeling that makes you feel ill, especially before public speaking. Don't worry, public speaking is one of the most common fears in the world. The public is bound by the common fear of speaking to the public.

WHAT ON EARTH IS SNOW?

Language is shaped by culture, traditions, history and even geography of a place.

Geography?

Let's take 'snow', for example. Any other word to replace snow that you or the thesaurus can think of? No?

The people on the northern fringes of the world are said to have a hundred or more names for snow.

Among the multiple languages spoken in the region, like Inuit in Greenland and Canada and Yupik in Alaska, several are compounding languages, which means sticking words together. So, while there may be a few base words for snow, there's a blizzard of words that describe various types of snow. Anthropologist Igor Krupnik compiled these words from ten Inuit dialects.

Here's where the geography comes in. It's a survival thing.

In the Inupiaq dialect of Wales, Alaska, be careful that the ice covering the sea isn't *auniq*, full of holes. Best you go out in *utuqaq*, perma-ice, which never melts, instead.

The Sami, who live in the extreme Russian and Scandinavian North, have hundreds of names for snow animals, including a thousand for reindeer. So, when you are asked which reindeer you want for your sleigh, be specific. *Leami* would get you a short, stout reindeer and *snarri*, a reindeer with short, stout antlers.

FROM 100 TO ZERO

Diametrically opposite, there are languages that have no word at all for snow. Why would they? It doesn't snow in that region. Tetum, a dialect on the Timor-Leste Island in Indonesia is one of these languages. But then, by that logic, we don't really have aliens, but we do have a word for them, don't we? And so, Tetum may soon get its own word for snow, because that's how words grow.

Would the people of the ice-covered northern climes have a word for hot sand? Or better still, for tiptoeing across hot sand? The Namibians have a precise word in Rukwangli for just that: *hanyauku*.

Break. Bite.
Bitter. Blacken.

How do you think most culture-bound words were born? Where would the word first be brought out to face the world? In a gathering of happy relatives and friends, cheering and raising toasts to the newborn word? Absolutely!

Each culture celebrates its uniqueness through customs and traditions, puzzling to outsiders, and has special names for them.

Chinese myth says Panhu, the dog god became human to marry a princess and gave her a gorgeous red phoenix dress, which is why brides in China wear red. P.S. Maybe I'm a dog god too?

WEDDING WORDS

Weddings are perfect places for unique rituals that get passed down from one generation to another, till most people realize they could never get married without having this . . . this . . . what's it called . . . ? What's the word for this thing we do?

Break it up

Polterabend in Germany happens on the day before the wedding. An evening or *abend* where *polten* or lots of noise is made. People bring old crockery, pots and vases and then throw them around and smash them. This sparks off sprees of singing and cheering till dawn. You don't have to take any presents, except for that old toilet bowl to crunch up there. The idea is that the couple will spend a long, long time cleaning up the mess, teaching them how to work together in the future.

Roce

In Goa, India, the *roce* ceremony happens the day before a Catholic wedding where the bride and groom are captured at their houses and doused with coconut milk in a purifying ritual. However, for a bit of fun, oil, beer, shampoo, flowers or eggs get added. The bride and groom are in such a mess that they can't leave the house until their wedding the next day.

134

Haldi

This Indian traditional ceremony before a Hindu wedding sees the bride and groom covered in turmeric paste and sandalwood mixed with milk or rosewater. A detox and glow combined, which will also ward off evil.

Blackening

In Scotland, the bride or groom gets tarred and feathered, in treacle, feathers and any other kind of muck before being carried with much hullaballoo to be thrown into the sea to clean up.

Clearly, none of these words would make sense in any other culture. You couldn't be screaming at someone anywhere else in the world to break plates or blacken the bride, could you?

Bitter

A word you'd only ever yell at a wedding in Russia. While toasting the couple, guests shout 'gorko' over and over. They're calling the food on the table bitter and coaxing the couple to kiss to sweeten the mood. Don't try it out anywhere else, though. This culture of calling the feast bitter, if used outside Russia, will be insulting enough to get you off the guest list, and out on the street, rather quickly.

Bite it!

You know how you cut your birthday cake and then your friends smash your face into it? Turns out that you can blame the Mexicans for that. La Mordida in Mexico is the smashing of your face into your cake while everyone yells *mordida*, meaning bite!

That's how words grow up in different parts of the world. If there isn't a word to describe a happening or habit or anything local, it gets made up. Some words stay within their cultures while others are shape-shifters that can easily morph into different languages.

Do you need many people to make up the word together or can one person do that alone?

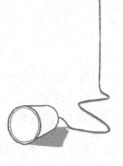

One-Man Words

It's funny, if you think of it. A writer uses a word that doesn't exist but describes exactly what they want to say. A reader scans the word and assumes it's just a word they haven't heard of before. 'Let me not act ignorant,' they might think and, in turn, use it with others. And just like that, a word is born and raised.

Here's a list of writers who have fattened up the English language with hundreds of words:

William Shakespeare

No 'champion', 'bandit', 'mountaineer' or 'madcap' would be roaming around our books without the Bard. Shakespeare is said to have coined 1,700 words that made it into our vocabularies and many more that didn't. What 'wappened'? Okay, so that's a word that didn't make it, but what fun it would have been!

Remember him the next time you find something 'laughable' or 'majestic' or 'gloomy' or 'zany'. He made up 'zany' in the sixteenth century? That's 'unreal'!

P.S. Many words are now credited to multiple sources and authors.

John Milton

Among Milton's many new words that slipped into English, here's one with a wicked backstory.

In *Paradise Lost*, from the seventeenth century, Milton described the capital city of Satan as one with all (*pan*) demons (*daimon*). Easy to see how the word pandemonium came to describe situations when all hell breaks loose.

Dr Seuss

My top vote for pulling words out of thin air goes to Dr Seuss, even though they didn't make it to a dictionary. The popular author of over sixty children's books is the master craftsman of nonsense words. What surprises grown-ups is how easily children give the non-word its own meaning. I mean, you'd have 'thunk' no one would know what it meant. But you read it 'once-ler' and you get it. With a 'hunk of chuck-a-luck', you will.

Whose Words Were These?

Fill in the blanks to find out who first came up with these words you use almost every day:

1. Tween: J _ _ TOL_ _ _ _

2. Nerd: DR S_ _ SS

3. Snark: _EWIS _ARROLL

4. Yahoo: JON_ _ _ _ _ SW_FT

5. Boredom: _HARLES _ICKENS

If that's how words spring up,
how do entire languages start?

TWISTS AND TURNS

You Tarzan, Me Jane

New languages spring up when people try to include other people in their communication. Or they spring up when you don't want to include other people. Confused?

She would have become leopard-dinner had the strange man in a loin cloth (a leopard-fur loin cloth, not a lion loin cloth) not swung in on the vines of a tree and saved her. Anyone familiar with *Tarzan of the Apes* knows what happens next. They must say something, but Jane Porter speaks only English, and he, well, he was raised by apes. After a few chest thumps and finger-pointing, he finally says, 'Me Tarzan. You Jane.'

Or not.

This is one of those long-lasting misquotes that merely sounds better than the original. It was never said in the original book by Edgar Rice Burroughs or in the first film based on the book. The actor quipped about it in an interview later, and it got misquoted ever after.

We're misquoting it here to introduce a way in which language is created. When people who speak different languages need to communicate, one group usually adapts and tries to adopt the other group's language, which is what cooks up a pidgin.

Pidgin is not a native language. Once the need to speak to each other is over, it dies out, or if it's strong enough to survive, it becomes a Creole.

Pidgin is not named after you, pigeon. It's derived from the word business in the language that Chinese merchants used to trade on the docks.

Creole could be a native language. It's a form of nativized pidgin when the kids in a community begin to speak in this newly created language. The Creole gets way more complex, with a grammar and structure and rules of its own. Malay has fourteen known Creole offshoots.

Creoles have been fighting a battle to get themselves recognized in the world of linguistic purists, and they're winning.

Tok Pisin, of Creole origins, is the most spoken language in Papua New Guinea today. Haiti has Haitian Creole. Some people in the Andaman speak a Hindustani Creole, and Bishnupriya is a Creole spoken in North East India and Bangladesh, descending from Bengali-Assamese and Manipuri. The people of Louisiana speak a French-flavoured Creole.

WE'RE SPEAKING WHAT?

The Middle English Creole Hypothesis proposes that what you and I are speaking or reading or writing right now is a Creole itself. English, it points out, is an amalgam of the languages of the Central French and Anglo-Norman speakers. *Quoi?*

You start a language to get people talking together. Why would anyone start a language meant to keep other people out?

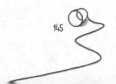

145

A Language
for Two

Poto and Cabengo are the names of twins. Names that the twins gave each other. In a language that they spoke only to each other. Which had sixteen different ways to say potato salad. None of which the adults taught them.

About forty per cent of twins invent words that only the other one understands. It's called Cryptophasia (from a Greek word for secret).

But, back to potato salad now.

CRYPTOPHASIA

Poto and Cabengo were what Grace and Virginia Kennedy called each other. To the world, they were the amazing twins who spoke in their own language. Their parents used to leave them with their grandmother, who used to remain busy with her own work.

In the twins' little world of two, they made up names for everything and their very own way of speaking. They threw in German words that their grandma spoke and English words that their parents spoke, and tossed them all together.

'*Snup-aduh ah-wee diedipana, dihabana.*'

When their babbling was discovered to be private communication, it caught the world's attention. Their parents even took them from city to city as a media act.

Give it up, you two!

Most twins who start out with Cryptophasia are weaned off it quickly. You know how twins are put in separate classes in school? That's to prevent them from jabbering only with each other.

When we're young, we love the idea of twinning. Dressing up like a bestie or making the same faces, etc. When I was a kid, like most kids, I wanted to be one of a pair of twins or triplets or quadruplets or quintuplets or more. However, my parents didn't share my enthusiastic vision of a football team of kids.

When names of friends become words

A quaint way of speaking popped up about a century ago in Boonville, a tiny community in a remote valley in California. Since the local people all knew each other, things were named after friends. The pay phone was called a Buckey Walter. (That was after Walter who owned the first phone, which costed a buck or a dollar per call.) Zachariah Clifton made a superb coffee, so a coffee was called a ZC or a Zeese, and so on. Outsiders, quite obviously, had no idea what these things were. In fact, it was so private that local soldiers used Boontling (which is what the language in Boonville came to be known as) to send secret messages during World War One.

**Heard of a language so special
that you can't hear it?**

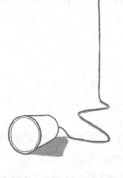

NSL: The Language No Adult Knew

It was only in 1977 that the hearing-challenged children of Nicaragua got to be 'heard'. The Nicaraguan government opened centres for special education in San Judas, Managua, and hundreds of children were enrolled. There was excitement and hope. The teachers were told to teach them lip-reading and Spanish. It didn't work out as smoothly as it was supposed to.

Then, something quite unexpected happened. As these things usually do. (If you expect the unexpected, does it become the expected?)

The children took their learning into their own hands (pun intended). This was the first time that so many deaf children had been together. They realized they didn't have to try and speak or hear or twist themselves into knots to enter the world of others. They could form their own way of communicating, and they did just that. Effortlessly, too. They began to sign to one another.

Over the years, as older students taught their special language to the newly enrolled kids, the language grew more complex. Nicaraguan Sign Language was officially accepted. It stunned the world. No adults had taught it to the kids. No adults even knew how to communicate as seamlessly as the kids did.

Four generations of students have been adding their own bits to the language and polishing it up. It has its own structure and grammar now and keeps getting more sophisticated. It is an example of the young teaching the old.

What about communication deliberately designed to be a secret?

Talking with the Devil

CYPHERS AND CODES

The first pictorial etchings were from 4,000 years ago. Were the hieroglyphics, or any of the ancient scripts, codes?

No.

They were known to 'their' people. It just took 'us' people ages to find out what they meant.

A code or cypher is designed to deliberately keep outsiders from understanding the message and is used cleverly in wars or espionage. I've dropped a few of the fun ones here.

Can You Atbash This?

Ready to crack one of the oldest codes? Atbash comes from Aleph Taw Bet Shin, letters in the Hebrew alphabet. It is a simple substitution cypher which can be used in any script.

Ready? All you need to do is write down the letters of the English alphabet in order. Now, below that, write the letters in reverse. You will have Z under the A, Y under the B, X under the C, and so on.

Now, decipher this:

GLL VZHB?

The Kamasutra code

Women's empowerment began way, way back in India. Consider this—a secret code given to women to communicate so that they could keep their secrets in the fourth century.

The *Kama Sutra* was compiled by the Brahmin scholar Vatsyayana in the fourth century CE. It empowered women to learn sixty-four different arts, like chess, perfume-making and carpentry. *Mlecchita vikalpa* was the art of secret-writing in codes that would keep their business strictly their business, the same rights of privacy that women are still fighting for now.

The Dorabella cipher

It was supposed to be a 'thank you', but the person being thanked didn't know she was being thanked because . . . well, it was in code.

Composed of what looks like a series of rotating m's in eighty-seven different characters, like the hands of a clock, it was meant as a note of thanks from the composer Sir Edward Elgar to his hosts, specifically their daughter, Dora, in 1897.

Was it the score for a musical piece? Much conjecture later, it still hasn't been cracked, making it one of the most secret pieces in the history of music . . . or thank yous . . . or m's.

The dancing men and Sherlock Holmes

There's nothing that the detective Sherlock Holmes couldn't crack. Not even a dance.

Once, Holmes was handed a puzzling note with dancing stick figures by a terrified couple. Notes like these were dropped in their garden. They had no clue what the dancing men meant but were naturally alarmed.

Now, Holmes wouldn't be Holmes if he had no clue, would he? And generations of story-readers wouldn't have a story. Holmes figured out the dancing men code—a substitution code—using a man to represent each letter of the alphabet.

He went on to encode a message in the same stick-figure code and sent it on to the murderer . . . can't give away the ending, can I?

Arthur Conan Doyle published *The Adventure of the Dancing Men* in 1903, calling it one of his favourite stories. No more spoilers. The idea of a book about language is that you go read more . . . and then some more.

The Choctaw code

'Little gun shoot fast'; few stories about wars are this charming.

During World War One, the US Army suspected the Germans were listening to their phone calls and cracking their most complex codes. They turned to the Choctaw Native Americans fighting alongside them, who began to communicate the messages to each other in their own dialects.

To make it even more confusing, the Choctaw Native Americans didn't use traditional military terms, but terms like 'Little gun shoot fast' for a machine gun. Translators didn't have the foggiest idea what they were on about.

Interestingly, help was sought once again from the Native Americans during World War Two. The Navajo code was the only one the most skilled code crackers admitted they couldn't crack.

The Mygurudu mystery

Sitting at a tea shop in Malappuram, Kerala, a young researcher, Pramod Irumbuzhi, overheard two elders speaking in a tongue he couldn't quite place. They admitted it was the secret Mygurudu code language created by the imprisoned freedom fighters of the 1921 Malabar Rebellion. As the jail wardens also spoke Malayalam, the prisoners came up with a secret code by swapping letters and sounds to pass on messages that left the wardens perplexed.

In the 1950s, Mygurudu became popular once again. Peasants used it to keep their landlords from understanding their conversations. It served well as a baffle-the-bosses code. Is that why more people, including youngsters, have been taking it up of late?

BAN CODING!

The German monk Johannes Trithemius wrote Polygraphia, a series of six books, in the 1500s. It was one of the earliest books on codes. It included Trithemius's inventions of the Changing Key cypher, Square Table and the Ave Maria cypher, which cleverly used Latin words instead of letters, therefore looking like a prayer. Nevertheless, suspicions were raised. The monk was expelled. People were convinced his codes were a way to talk to the devil. The alphabet he introduced, which came to be known as the Witches' Alphabet, is still used in modern witchcraft today.

There was something dark and devious about cryptography. Today, cyber security works via many encryption techniques, and the codes themselves are created by scientific minds. But back then, this whole hidden, little understood thing began to be considered one of the dark arts—a shady, sinister black world.

THE BLACK CHAMBERS

The Black Chambers, staffed with crafty codebreakers, sprang up across European cities in the 1700s. One of the most infamous and smoothly oiled ones was in Vienna.

At the crack of dawn, the mail coming into foreign embassies in Austria was spirited away to the Black Chamber, where a bunch of people got down to work immediately. They melted the seals, opened and copied all the private documents, then resealed them and sent them on to the embassies—all this before the workday would officially begin. At one point, this chamber even sold spy information to other countries. Black business indeed!

Around 250,000 carrier pigeons were used in wars to carry messages in code. Some codes haven't been cracked till now.

What came first? The language or the speaker? (Since no one's cracked the chicken or egg till now.)

The Language of No Country

If you believe that a group of people began to chatter among themselves and it grew more refined over time into a language, you're right. If you believe that a language is first created and then goes looking for speakers, you're talking about a conlang or a constructed language.

So, you're right, too, in a way. There's space for all sorts of beliefs.

Conlang vs Conlangs

Though conlangs have been around for thousands of years, the term conlang only came up recently. Many people have been taking shots at constructing new languages, with varying degrees of success, for hundreds of years. However, the word conlang for constructed languages was first noticed in a post in 1991. The conlangs didn't know they were called conlangs before that.

Wordless Conlang

In the fifteenth century, Italian jesters who took their act to different countries, where they couldn't speak the local languages, made up an onomatopoeic performance that was a combination of mime-mimicry and dumb-charades to perform on stage. The grunt-groan-squeak-scream format called Grammelot was made famous by the Nobel-winning Italian writer Dario Fo. It is practised by many mime artists and performers in some form even today.

The conlangs that created worlds

J.R.R. Tolkien invented his first languages, Animalic and Nevbosh when he was thirteen. Yes, Tolkien who wrote *The Lord of the Rings* and *The Hobbit* stories.

'The stories were made rather to provide a world for the languages . . . to me a name comes first and the story follows,' Tolkien said.

He based his conlangs on the languages he had studied, including some ancient ones like Old Icelandic, Welsh and Old Norse. He went the whole way, even inventing scripts for each.

Fan clubs all over the world today don't just train in but go on to have competitions in the languages that Tolkien invented, such as Elvish, Mannish, Dwarvish, Entish language families . . . oh and, not to forget, Black Speech.

NaMarie, for now. We're moving on from Middle Earth.

The conlangs that aliens speak

Klingon is spoken by a species of aliens in *Star Trek* and by thousands of Trekkie fans ever since. Linguist Marc Okrand was brought on deck to develop the language for the series in the 1980s. Today, Klingon boasts a dictionary, a Klingon Language Institute, magazines and films. Those aliens can apparently spout poetry. I know *pagh* about it, which is zero in Klingon (a dash and not an oval). So, I guess I know *wa'* word, then?

The conlang created for snakes in Harry Potter's world is Parseltongue. You have to be a wizard to speak that. Look up 'Doggic', though. A conlang with its own vocabulary and rules. But you have to be a dog to speak that.

The contest-winning conlang

The *Game of Thrones* producers held a contest to choose someone to create the language for their series out of the few words scattered around the George R.R. Martin books. David J. Peterson contested. He spent eighteen hours a day working out a complex grammar and vocabulary for his language. It paid off. He won the competition and created Dothraki.

Dothraki has fourteen words for horse. (Nowhere as many as the Sami have for reindeer.) But try and find a word for throne in the language of the *Game of Thrones*. No?

A blockbuster Indian conlang

A tsunami of terrifying guttural clicks announces that the fearsome warriors from the Kalakeya tribes are close by. They plot to attack the Mahishmathi kingdom, in a tongue known only to them—Kiliki. Its creator had called his original language Cliq.

This fear-inducing language was constructed by Madhan Karky for the blockbuster films of Baahubali. It has twenty-two symbols which have given rise to about 3,000 words, at last count. Forty grammar rules govern how you speak it. It has its own app and website which was launched on International Mother Tongue Day in 2020. There's a killer feature on the website—type in your name and see it in Kiliki script. Go on. A few clicks will get you there.

The superhit films were released in several languages. Waiting for the version in Kiliki itself. That would be kilikool!

The most successful conlang

In 1887, Ludwig Zamenhof created a language which came to be called Esperanto, after his pen name, Dr Esperanto, which meant Dr Hopeful. The hope was for a more equal world. If everyone spoke the same language, 'ideals, convictions, aims would be the same too'.

'Everyone the same?' Hitler howled, and Stalin stormed. 'No superior race (which, of course, is our race)? Off with you!' Esperanto speakers found themselves in jails and concentration camps.

Despite attempts to shut it down, Esperanto survived. Today, the internet has given it a boost. There are clubs devoted to conversing in the language every day. Google and Facebook started Esperanto versions. It's an easy language to learn—sixteen basic rules—and anyone can learn it. If you'd like to be a world citizen where no one is a foreigner or outsider, come on over. *Bonvenon!*

**If new languages are popping up,
are others dying out?**

Waking up
Sleeping Languages

The going, going, gone quiz

1. A language disappears every:

    a. two weeks   c. two months

    b. one month

2. Since 1950, the number of languages that have died out are over:

    a. 120   c. 510

    b. 230

3. By the next century, the portion of endangered languages that will not survive is:

    a. All   c. 50-90%

    b. 0-50%

4. 1/3rd of the world's languages has less than:

    a. 100 speakers   c. 10,000 speakers

    b. 1,000 speakers

5. The number of languages that are only spoken and have no writing to record them is:

a. 2,000   c. 800

b. 1,000

Answer key:

1a. A language disappears every two weeks. Languages are disappearing even while you read this book on language.

2b. Over 230 languages will never be heard again.

3c. Depending on the help they get or not, 50-90% of endangered languages will vanish.

4b. A thousand or less people still speak 33% of the world's remaining languages, and these speakers are growing older.

5a. Two thousand languages have not been written, and so when the last person who speaks the language dies, the language will too.

There's never bad news without a whisper of good in the air. Every cloud has a silver lining. Every week ends with a holiday. Every burnt cake has some yummy crumbs you're going to be allowed to scrape off. And every endangered species has someone willing to save it.

While institutes and societies for the preservation of languages do brilliant work tirelessly, the job has also been taken up by a few people too stubborn to let their language die. Some of the more unique attempts to drag a language out while it was sinking, or at times, even after it was sunk, follow.

You've got to love cake, tigers or a forgotten language enough to save them. And you'll find a way.

One man and a radio: Ōlelo Hawai'i

What can I do? You shrug. Languages dying, pollution rising, glaciers melting, exams getting tougher. Rotten! But what can I do? I'm just one person.

Larry Kimura was one person who pulled an entire language out of its near-death experience. If there were only scattered groups of native speakers of this Hawaiian tongue, how could their voices be heard by all? He set up a small studio in a tall building in Waikiki, Hawaii, where he started a radio show in the 1970s. Kimura began to get any native speakers he could find—speaking. The lilts of this almost submerged tongue went out on the airwaves.

As the movement grew, activists looked to the youngest— the preschoolers. Punana Leo, the nest of voices, opened with one school which taught in Hawaiian and has multiplied to over twenty. Thousands of people on the islands speak Hawaiian today: the old stories, songs, dances and *oli* or the chants.

A village which sings: Sanskrit

Near the peaceful river Tunga lies the farming village of Mattur in Shivamogga district. The villagers speak of their village as being gifted by King Krishnadevaraya to the Vedic scholars of the period.

Like other villages in Karnataka, Mattur has fields, small houses shoulder to shoulder, narrow mud lanes, plenty of trees and the chattering of children at play. Like other villages in Karnataka, people speak Kannada except when they sometimes break into Sanskrit. And that is no coincidence. Aware that a language only thrives through daily use, Sanskrit was made compulsory in the *paathashaala*, the school in the village. The dog ate your homework? Well, learn to say that in Sanskrit, and you're excused.

The temple in the centre of Mattur, surrounded by brightly painted houses, resounds with the sound of *shlokas* that are thousands of years old. The school reverberates with the chants of ten-year-olds learning the Vedas. The *gataka* tradition uses storytelling in song to make long-forgotten stories and poetry come alive once more.

Almost all the residents in the Sanskrit Village can do their groceries, chat through the afternoon or exchange gossip in classical Sanskrit. Still, the real proof is plastered on some graffiti on the walls (which we hope someone won't whitewash), probably the only Sanskrit graffiti anywhere in the world. Proof that the next generation of Sanskrit speakers is here.

The Inca rap: Quechua

The Inca kings spread their language across the settlements of the mountainous Andes in the fifteenth century. Over forty-five dialects emerged, but generations later, they have all but trickled away. The older native speakers will carry their speech with them to other worlds. The younger generation won't speak it. Or will they? Perhaps they will sing it?

Quechua was only a spoken language and was discredited as backward or uncool by Spanish speakers. Kids who spoke it were bullied at school.

Not done! The young took up the tune, alongside the Quechua book fairs and radio shows. They made sure that the Quechua blues and rap not only wafted across the internet but also echoed once more in the mountains where the Inca once reigned supreme.

The child who spoke a 2,000-year-old language: Hebrew

How could you speak Hebrew? It was forbidden. It was too sacred for daily use.

The result? Though it survived in written form, the last native speaker died, and so did the spoken language.

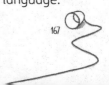

Many centuries passed. Then, in 1881, Eliezer Ben-Yehuda threw himself wholly into the revival of Hebrew that was seeing much interest at the time. He began work on its first dictionary and even raised his own son as the first native Hebrew speaker in 2,000 years.

Multiple efforts from various people took Hebrew, extinct since the fourth century BCE, to the official language of Israel today. From officially dead to official.

A pretty chatbot: Ainu

Their homes echoed with the laughter of children and the growls of bears. Wait . . . what? Bears and kids under one roof?

The Ainu worshipped the spirit of the Sacred Bear. They brought bear cubs home and raised them alongside their own families.

These unique traditions, along with their various dialects, went almost extinct. Almost. During the Meiji era, the Ainu were driven to the north-eastern islands of Japan (now called Land of the Ainu), where their culture and language were almost stamped out. Almost.

Today, the Ainu, who are left with almost no native speakers (it is a language isolate with no known family), have begun to pick up the threads of what they once had. A very determined individual helps them out with this, and she's not even alive. We're not getting into ghost stories here, though the spirits of the land may urge us to. AI Pirika is a natural language processing app that functions as a chatbot. Named Pirika, which translates in Ainu as pretty girl, the virtual agent, it's hoped, will get more people speaking in the language of the People of the Sacred Bear.

The Only Speakers of Maypure Are Parrots

The parrot squawked and screeched, but no one understood a word. Explorer Alexander Von Humboldt, on his journey through the Orinoco River, South America, in 1799, found a parrot with the Carib Indian tribe, which spoke an alien language. Though they had kept the parrot alive, the tribe had driven the neighbouring tribespeople to extinction—every last one of them. Not a very neighbourly thing to do. It didn't take the explorer long to realize that the parrot had picked up what the slain people had been speaking, making it the last living being to speak Maypure.

Conscious of the treasure he held in his hands, Von Humboldt immediately got down to recording the parrot's words–a language that would otherwise be lost. No one speaks the language now. Birds still do.

Almost 200 years later, artist Rachel Berwick, fired up by the story, created an art installation–an aviary in which she kept Amazon parrots she'd trained using the Maypure recordings. These are the only eight surviving speakers of Maypure, all of them parrots.

From bears and parrots to the mouse.

Do humans need to survive for our languages to? We now have machines to keep language on life support. Artificial intelligence systems can write poetry, fabricate school essays, discuss political theories, solve problems and have long conversations. Reassuring or threatening?

P.S. This book was not written by a chatbot. Just saying.

Can anyone reveal what language will be like in the future? Short answer: no. Long answer: in the following section.

TECH-TALK
AND
TOMORROW

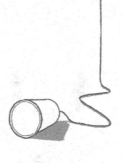

De Vices
over De Years

Smoke signals fizzled out in the rain, and pigeon mail was risky if an eagle took an interest in your pigeon. At that point in time, machines were considered more predictable. They wouldn't disappear on you (though mine often go on the blink and stop talking to me).

A quick run-through of the long history of communication devices:

Semaphore telegraph: Instant long-distance communication farther than the voice could carry? How? The semaphore telegraph was one of the most ambitious machines of communication over long distances in the eighteenth century. The structure set up on the peaks of hills, up to twenty miles apart, looked like a windmill with gigantic arms which pointed in specific directions to signal messages. These messages were picked up via telescopes on other peaks of other hills and passed on.

Signals at Sea

How this book could help you if shipwrecked (the risk of which is 0.0001%).

The flag semaphore is used for emergency signalling at sea. Even today, flags, paddles or your arms can spell out a message by following the alphabet on the opposite page.

Tip: Your arms go clockwise.

Telegraph: Many inventors simultaneously created their versions of the telegraph across different countries in the 1830s and 1840s. The device transmitted electric signals over a wire between points. Samuel Morse went on to create the code used by the telegraph in dots and dashes, the famous Morse code.

Try this: Figure out how to spell your name in Morse code and then rap it out on the dining table; to annoy an annoying sibling.

Telephone: A race once again, this time to claim the first telephone. Though different inventors had come up with similar ways to send sound over distances, Alexander Graham Bell filed the first patent for his device, which could turn sound into electricity and then again into sound. In 1875, he made the world's first telephone call and said, 'Mr Watson, come here. I want you.'

Try this: Look up an image of the first telephone in history. Looks like they're speaking into a sewing machine, doesn't it? Erm . . . you may have to look up an image of a sewing machine, too, in case you've never seen one.

Radio: Nikola Tesla demonstrated his wireless radio in 1893. But it was the Italian inventor Guglielmo Marconi who built a wireless telegraph system in 1895 and patented it. When his radio worked across the room, he tried it across his garden, then a kilometre and, finally, several kilometres across the Atlantic Ocean.

Cellular telephone: 'The telephone number should be a person rather than a location' was what drove Martin Cooper to invent 'the brick'. The brick? That was the nickname fondly given to the first cellular phone. This first hand-held phone, The DynaTAC, made by Motorola in 1973, was over a kilogram in weight and about the size of a book. It burnt a hole in your pocket in more ways than one.

World Wide Web: The first webpage ever was a page on how to create web pages. Rather helpful of Tim Berners-Lee, who introduced this first webpage in 1991. He further developed HTML, URLs, HTTP and the other things we take for granted today. His idea was to get computers to start talking to each other. And to get people talking to each other through computers which were already talking to each other.

Try this: See if you can get on to the URL of the first website. Try sitting down for this: at a rough estimate, today, about 175 websites are created every minute! No wonder it's so tough to find information that's relevant. If you do get the information at 11,000 hits of different answers for any question, you still don't know which one is right.

Email: The first email was sent to a computer in the same room. (We all stand guilty of doing that till today.) In 1971, Ray Tomlinson sent the first email to himself. He says, 'The test messages were entirely forgettable, and I have, therefore, forgotten them.' Honest. He says he probably ran his finger across the top line of the keyboard. (Without looking at your keyboard, do you know the ten letters on the top line?) Tomlinson also came up with the '@', 'from', 'subject' and 'date' we use on email.

Duckling@Monkey

The email sign @, which is the only new sign added to Morse code since the First World War, has entertaining names in other languages because of the way it looks.

- Polish: *malpa* (monkey)

- Taiwan Chinese: *xiao laoshu* (mouse)

- Hungarian: *kukac* (worm)

- Greek: *papaka* (duckling)

- German: *klammeraffe* (spider monkey)

- Finnish: *miukumauku* (miaow!)

- Slovak: *zavinac* (pickled fish)

I'm voting for Armenian. Their word for @ is *ishnik*, which means puppy.

Instant message: The first instant message, sent on AOL by Ted Leonsis to his wife in 1993 was seriously sweet. 'Don't be scared . . . it is me. Love you and miss you.'

Chatbot: Eliza was born in 1966. Joseph Weizenbaum created the chatbot to respond by matching words in a question to ready-made responses. Eliza's creator was troubled because people were confiding their deepest secrets in her. She wasn't human, he insisted, and never would be. Chatbots are artificial intelligence programmes which pop up and give you information, answer questions or, often, confuse you totally.

A series of chatbots followed Eliza, such as ALICE, Alexa, Siri, Zootopia bot (especially for kids), and even chatbots to help you when either you or your device has a breakdown; bots to help you with bots. If you want to know more, ask ChatGPT, who, once again, I remind you, is not writing this book.

P.S. I asked ChatGPT if it could write a book and this was its answer: 'I, as an AI language model, don't possess personal experiences, intentions, or consciousness, so I can't author a book.'

What's next? What do we create next?

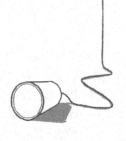

Get the
World Talking

We don't know what's coming up. That's the exciting bit. Technology is shaping our world rapidly. One of the main goals, for example, is to enable people from all over the planet to talk to each other.

New words and bridge words would enter languages. Translations would be available for whomever you're speaking to. Machines would talk for us—my machine would talk to your machine.

A WORD YOU WON'T KNOW TILL TOMORROW

Despite a language being around for eons, it keeps fattening up with the 'in' words and shedding the 'out' words. Each new generation adds new words that would have made no sense a century ago. A few obvious sources:

From tech: words like autocorrect and screenshot. Inbox me, and I'll tell you more.

From young people like you: Sus. Gaming it. Lol! Sus, for suspicious, has been around from the 1960s! Ikr?

From other languages: Among the recent additions to the Oxford English Dictionary, for example, are shaadi, dabba and hartal. Let's hope one didn't lead to the next.

From new meanings for old words: Today, home, enter, tab, escape, window, mouse, refresh—all mean what they didn't start out meaning. A stressed-out friend told me how she had quarantined her kid at home all day for playing all of the previous day instead of studying. While passing his room, she heard him yell, 'Escape!' Oh no, you won't, she thought, marching in, only to find him playing an online video game.

From events, like the pandemic: Coronials, quaranteens, vaxication and infodemic.

Eat Your
Meal Sideways

Augmented reality glasses that translate multiple languages were recently presented at 2023 tech fairs across the world. They claim to translate in real-time whichever language the person opposite you is speaking. There are apps to translate images from other scripts.

It may be fun to have a quick look at some words that may stump the artificial (most) intelligent. These words will stay in their respective mother tongues because they are the non-translatables.

Hyppytyynytyydytys: I want to start with a favourite. Tough to translate and tougher to pronounce, this word means to enjoy bouncing on a bouncy cushion in Finnish, the language, not the end. Did you happen to notice that it's a really long word without vowels?

Yoko meshi: Japanese for saying that speaking a foreign language is way too complex. It's like eating your meal sideways.

Gilchi: In Korea, Gilchi is someone stupid who is always getting lost.

Suilk: Scottish for the slobbering sound you make while eating, drinking or lapping up something. No suilking or sulking at the table!

Zhaghzhagh: Persian for your teeth chattering because you're either freezing or furious. Test it out. It's onomatopoeic for the sound you actually make.

Pana po'o: Hawaiians have the funniest observations. This is when you're scratching your head, hoping that will help you remember something . . . did it work?

Epibreren: Dutch for when you're actually doing nothing (or nothing good), but you're pretending to be so, so busy. Guilty?

Backpfeifengesicht: German for a face that just asks to be slapped. Ouch!

Bombaat: That's colloquial Kannada for awesome!

Gondogol: Bangla for something fishy going on. Of course, Bengalis love fish, so that's probably not the right translation because *gondogol* means trouble.

Having fun so far?

Chindi chitranna: It means lemon rice in Kannada but has been filtered down to mean super fun.

Pisan zapra: Malay for how long it takes to eat a banana. Apparently, it's two minutes. How long would you take?

Poronkusema: Once an official unit of time, this absolutely hilarious Sami word in Finland measures how long a reindeer can run before taking a pee break. Seven-and-a-half kilometres is what someone has measured it to be. I wonder who did this most precise and interesting measuring. And now I'll bet you're wondering too.

Age-otori: Japanese for a haircut that makes you look worse than you did before. I can't see this word without laughing, because I've had so many *age-otori* haircuts that I thought would turn out sleek and, well, they didn't. Quite the opposite.

Susegaad: If you love going to Goa, this could be why. This is the word for what the Goans call the laidback attitude of relaxing and loving life.

Ghodar deem: Horse egg . . . a what now? Obviously not possible. It's the Bangla way of telling you that it's a useless proposition, a lost hope.

Want to know more? Still have questions?

Pochemuchka! Russian for a kid who just keeps asking why.

Will there ever be a way for human beings everywhere to communicate? Sometime in the distant future, maybe?

All dogs across the world understand each other. Just saying. Or just barking.

The Future of Speaking: Thinking?

Let's end the talking book on a no-talking note.

What if we had one common way of communicating which everyone in the world could understand?

While the race is already on using Natural Language Processing and translation software, the last stop would be to tap directly into our brains.

You don't need to speak. Your thoughts will be picked up and translated to the receiver.

Does that sound like a dream . . . or a nightmare?

If there is a fear of data hacking today, imagine your brain being open to hacking. Your thoughts are not going to be private ever again. Your mother is going to know you're planning to fake a tummy ache to skip the test. Your teacher is going to know your dog didn't eat your homework. If you're angry, sad, jealous or hopeful but don't want to show any of that, too bad. Your brain is already telling them what you're thinking.

It could make for a dystopian science-fiction plot—or a magical utopian one in which injured people who've lost their speech can think it across to you.

FUTURE COMMUNICATION IN THE PRESENT

The 2014 World Cup in Brazil was kicked off by twenty-nine-year-old Juliano Pinto, a paraplegic man who kicked his way to a whole new record. This young volunteer was fitted into a robotic exoskeleton controlled by the brain, which was made by a team of over 100, led by Dr Miguel Nicolelisar. It is a step in the Walk-Again Project which we hope will see more successes in brain control.

Dr Rajesh Rao, Director, Centre of Neurotechnology and Professor at University of Washington, is doing some of the most exciting work in brain computer interfaces. He demonstrated his colleague Andrea Stocco and himself playing a video game. One of them saw the attack on-screen and thought about the best time to fire—just thought about it. Through their technology, the other received the magnetic impulse that made his hand press the key and fire it did.

There's even talk of implanting microchips in brains, as in Elon Musk's Neuralink. The chip will record neural activity and translate it to a computer that promises to get people who are injured or disabled moving again.

These are just some of the studies and projects being done today. Every time someone thinks or remembers or feels anything, electric signals zoom over the neurons in their brain. Scientists have been working on catching those signals and decoding them, then using them to learn how the brain acts when it thinks.

Brain to computer or, at some stage, brain to brain communication lends itself to all sorts of possibilities. Sci-fi, look out. We're catching up!

Tell Your Own Story

After travelling (with Marco and me) the long, winding path that language took, you could end this book with your own idea of what language will be in the future.

Here's a starter scenario to let your imagination go wild.

I KNOW WHAT YOU'RE SAYING

The school bell flags off the usual cacophony of students pouring out of the school gates. You too have stepped out on to the street, waiting for your father to drive up and take you home. He is in the Foreign Service and always travelling. But today, he's in town and has promised to pick you up.

You see two men rushing over, their faces anxious. One holds out his hand and says, 'We're here to take you home.

Your father's been in an accident.' He has a strange accent, this man. He's clearly a foreigner, but you've been used to meeting many of your father's foreign colleagues.

Your heart begins to pound. Is your father okay? What happened? Then, you shake your head. You've been told that it's too dangerous to go with a stranger. 'I think I'll wait for my father to call me.'

'He's in the hospital. He can't call,' the man insists, looming over you and reaching out for your bag strap. 'That's why he sent us. Come, quick. It's urgent.'

You back away. The man turns to his companion and begins to whisper hoarsely in a foreign language. You reach into your bag and slip on your headphones. Your father had brought you these live-translation headphones from a tech fair.

What will you hear? Is your father in trouble or are you? You lean in to get closer, to know what they're saying, and . . .

THE READING I DID BEFORE WRITING THIS BOOK

The research for this book runs into another ten books, with no talking dog for company either. Instead, I'll give you a brief run-through of what I read to pick out the exciting, essential stories for you. I chased stories deep into some delightfully detailed books, so let's start with those.

1. *A History of Language*—Steven Roger Fischer, Reaktion Books.

2. *A Little Book of Language*—David Crystal, Yale University Press.

3. *The Geography of Words: Vocabulary and Meaning in the World's Languages*—Danko Sipka, Cambridge University Press.

4. *The Unfolding of Language: The Evolution of Mankind's Greatest Invention*—Guy Deutscher, Arrow Books.

5. *Eats, Shoots & Leaves: The Zero Tolerance Approach to Punctuation*—Lynn Truss, HarperCollins.

6. *Linguistic Diversity*—David Nettle, Oxford University Press.

7. *Encyclopaedia of Indian Literature*—Sahitya Akademi.

8. *The Atlas of Unusual Languages: An exploration of language, people and geography*—Zoran Nikolic, HarperCollins.

9. *The Seeds of Speech: Language Origin and Evolution*—Jean Aitchinson, Cambridge University Press.

10. *The Power of Babel: A Natural History of Language*—John McWhorter, Harper Perennial.

After raving about language in the tech age, it's a no-brainer that I had to deep dive into the internet. I used various sources for each snippet you read, trying to check them against one another. Here are a few of the online resources I dipped into the most.

- **Magazines and websites of science publications**: www.psychologytoday.com, www.livescience.com, www.sciencedirect.com, www.scientificamerican.com, www.csmonitor.com

- **Articles published by sources in the social sciences**: www.britannica.com, www.nationalgeographic.com, www.guinnessworldrecords.com, www.history.com, www.worldhistory.org, www.livehistoryindia.com, www.nature.com, www.worldatlas.com

- **Government portals**: www.censusindia.gov.in, www.nasa.gov, www.education.gov.in, www.india.gov.in, www.nationalmuseumindia.gov.in, www.britishmuseum.org, www.ignca.gov.in

- **Organizations for the study of languages**: www.sanskrit.nic.in, www.linguisticsociety.org, www.babble.com, www.bilingual.io, www.dictionary.com, www.merriam-webster.com

- **Archives of news sites**: www.theguardian.com, www.thehindubusinessline.com, www.bbc.com, www.smithsonianmag.com, www.washingtonpost.com, www.newindianexpress.com, www.dw.com, www.indiatimes.com, www.theintrepidguide.com

- **Websites of foundations**: www.darwinproject.ac.uk, www.shuddhanandabharati.ch, www.harappa.com

Many historians heartily disagree with each other, of course, but learning different viewpoints was fun. And I hope that after reading *The Talking Book*, you can talk to others about it. Your opinion matters.

ACKNOWLEDGEMENTS

The first person I talked to about *The Talking Book* was Sohini Mitra, and she championed it right from the time it was a whimsical what-if. Thanks to her team at Penguin Random House: Simran Kaur, my hearteningly encouraging editor, and Shabari Choudhury, who went over each line with a fine-tooth comb and a suggestion and followed up with calls. The quirky cover owes its swag to Samar Bansal and to Siddhi Vartak who also gave my mascot, Marcopolo, in the inner pages, a keen attitude. Thank you to Mansi Shetty for the nifty marketing ideas and to the sales teams for the hard work once the book leaves shore.

I am indebted to the entire ecosystem that makes it possible for us to write and speak about our books. The literary fest organizers, bookstores and organizers of workshops for children—Archana Atri, Shyamala Shanmugasundaram, Funky Rainbow and Mita Kapur, my feisty literary agent. To fellow writers for feedback and support: Asha Nehemiah, Venita Coelho, Vaishali Shroff and Andaleeb Wajid. To the teachers, researchers and friends of friends to whom I reached out to get their perspectives on the stories here. To Abir Rautela, Ananya Sherpuri and my first young readers, thanks for their wise, old feedback. And the lion's share of my gratitude goes to my family for being mine.

Read More by the Author

SUPERZERO

Jane De Suza

Want to know how to be a superhero?

It's easy-peasy-choco-cheesy! But SuperZero, our ten-year-old hero, is the only student at the Superhero School who can't seem to find his superpowers. Every time he tries to save the town, he turns it upside down!

But when the Eggstremely Dangerous Eggster unleashes a truly diabolical weapon of mass destruction, it's left to SuperZero to foil his plans. Except, he's accidentally locked himself up in a zoo. Now . . . what to do?

Join SuperZero as he trips, tumbles and crashes through loony adventures with a vampire who hates blood, a dude who appears only in patches, a cutie who starts as a girl and ends as a snake, and a dog that eats everything in sight.

Read More by the Author

SUPERZERO AND THE CLONE CRISIS

Jane De Suza

With great trouble come great laughs!

After two crazy adventures, the peskiest . . . sorry, super-est superkid in town has now fallen **PLONK THUD crash** into a third.

Everyone including BigaByte, is in a lousy mood because someone's stealing their laughs? Whaaa?

Plus, SuperZero's mom has a bewildering surprise for him.

Plus, plus, plus there is a cunning clone in school who's turning himself into everyone else and creating full-on chaos. (Pssst, that's your cue, SuperZero. Do your thing!)

So much trouble can only be good news for SuperZero fans. Here come the hahas and high action once again.

WHEN THE WORLD WENT DARK

Jane De Suza

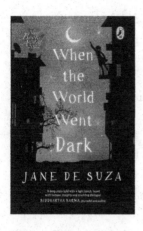

To help Swara, you'd have to dive into her world during the lockdown. Feel the almost-nine-year-old's heart break as she loses her favourite person ever, Pitter Paati. Swara pursues clues to find her, but stumbles upon a crime instead. VExpectedly, no one believes her.

Will Swara and her VAnnoying friends from the detective squad find the Ruth of the Matter in time?

Told with humour and sparkle, this compassionate story is about finding light in the darkest times of our lives. It packs in an intriguing mystery and even a good belly laugh. (Wait, is it OK to laugh?)

Read More by the Author

FLYAWAY BOY

Jane De Suza

Kabir doesn't fit in. Not in the wintry hill town he lives in, and not in his school, where the lines are always straight. Backed into a corner with no way out, Kabir vanishes.

With every adult's nightmare now coming true, finding this flyaway boy will mean understanding who he really is. Or is it too late?

Spirited and powerfully imaginative, *Flyaway Boy* is a story about embracing everything that makes you uniquely you.